M000187259

THE AMISH COWBOY'S BRIDE

MONTANA MILLERS

AMISH COWBOYS OF MONTANA
BOOK THREE

ADINA SENFT

Moonshell
Books

The Amish Cowboy's Bride / Adina Senft—1st ed.

ISBN: 978-1-950854-43-1 R101223

❦ Created with Vellum

PRAISE FOR ADINA SENFT

"Filled with spiritual insights and multilayered story-lines. At times readers will be chuckling and other times, misty eyed as the book unfolds."

— AMISH READER ON *HERB OF GRACE*

"A heart-warming tale that celebrates the best things about being Amish."

— CHRISTIAN FICTION ADDICTION ON *KEYS OF HEAVEN*

"Adina Senft has once again produced a simply sweet and engaging Amish romance novel, filled with twists and turns, enjoyable beyond compare."

— AMISH READER ON *BALM OF GILEAD*

"The first thing I loved about this story from Adina Senft is that it's set in Montana—we don't get many Amish stories set on the Western side of the US, so it was fun to sorta shift gears from farming to ranching. The Montana landscape in winter is an added bonus! I also loved that this is a prequel to her Montana Millers series, the origin story, if you will, of the Circle M Ranch and the love story that accompanies it. This story is a girl-next-door romance with layered characters and an overall sweetness to the tone that warms the heart."

— READING IS MY SUPERPOWER ON *THE AMISH COWBOY'S CHRISTMAS*

IN THIS SERIES

AMISH COWBOYS OF MONTANA

The Montana Millers

For Georgina, Adeline, and Kate—
three generations of strong, smart women

෧

"I will both lay me down in peace, and sleep:
for thou, Lord, only makest me dwell in safety."

— PSALM 4:8

THE AMISH COWBOY'S BRIDE

CHAPTER 1

MOUNTAIN HOME, MONTANA

Early April

*R*ebecca Miller had read somewhere that April was the cruelest month, and she could readily believe it. April delighted in teasing you—showing you the thickets of pussy willows all grey and furry down in the river bottom, the snow melting, the sky softening to a sweet blue. Spring was just around the corner, for sure and certain. And then winter would ride down the mountains like a thundering herd of wild mustangs, bowling you over and making you run for shelter. And coating the poor pussy willows in ice.

As a little girl, she had once come into the house crying, her mittened hands full of branches with their little grey buds. She was trying to save as many as she could from a freeze, as though they had been real kittens. Mamm had been so kind, putting the branches in pretty vases and explaining that their furry coats kept the willow tassels safe and warm until the sun told them it was time to come out.

Her fraternal twin sister Malena, of course, had immediately pulled a bud off a branch, sliced it open with a fingernail, and investigated to see if that were true. Rebecca had burst into tears all over again and Mamm's good work in calming her down had been undone in a moment.

But that was Malena for you. She liked to know how things worked. To be the one people paid attention to as she told them how things worked. The first word out of her mouth after *Mamm* and *Dat* and *neh* had been *why*.

The first word out of Rebecca's mouth had been ... well, Mamm said she hadn't talked as early as Malena, and when she finally got around to it, it was in short sentences, not single words. But by then it was too late. People had got used to listening to Malena, and looking mildly surprised when Rebecca spoke up or had an opinion about anything.

And now April had fooled them all again. She and Sara Fischer had gone to Sara's hay farm this morning to muck out the area that had once been the vegetable garden. They'd spent the day together, pulling up blackberry brambles and mulleins, and enjoying the lunch they'd packed. Rebecca's younger brother Joshua had joined them after his day's work as an apprentice to John Cooper, the *Englisch* saddle maker. He'd collected Sara in his own buggy, and the two of them had gone home to the Circle M and baby Nathan. Rebecca had a little more she wanted to finish in the garden, but then she'd hitched up Hester and set out for home, too.

Sara's hay farm was a fair distance from the Circle M Ranch on a nice day. When the clouds settled in and the temperature dropped, when the snow started to fall not in nice soft flakes, but in stinging bits of ice, then it seemed so far away it might as well be in Colorado.

Colorado.

No, she would not think about Colorado.

Because then she would think about *him*, and she'd spent far more nights dreaming about him already than was good for her. *Der gut Gott*, it appeared, did not have him in mind as Rebecca Miller's future husband, and no amount of mooning and dreaming and—let's be honest—praying about it was going to change the situation.

She'd seen him at singings and several volleyball and baseball games during her visit to Amity last summer. She'd never spoken to him. She knew his name—Andrew King—thanks to Amanda King, who was his niece by marriage in one of those flukes where the uncle was the same age as his nieces and nephews. The exact situation her baby sister was going to be in when she made her appearance any day now.

But back to Andrew King. Rebecca abandoned her pretense of not thinking about him. The truth was, she thought about him constantly.

She knew he preferred pie to cake. He had reddish-brown hair and strong shoulders and lips to die for and a big laugh. He was a carpenter by trade. He hadn't joined church, but Amanda said he had a good heart and that would bring him into the fold sooner or later. He was a year older than Rebecca, and was what the Amish considered *wild*. Which could mean anything from driving a car to talking in church. Anyway, that was the sum total of Rebecca's knowledge.

It wasn't much.

But it was everything she needed to fall head over heels in love.

He didn't need to know she had a crush on him the size of Montana. That would only invite teasing and jokes and even now, Rebecca would die if her sister and four brothers got wind of it. So she had filled her heart with the sight of him from across the room, which was a good thing, because when the next singing came around, he'd gone.

Gone. Without a good-bye, and without knowing how she felt.

Probably a blessing on both counts.

But still.

She flapped the reins over Hester's back. "Better hurry, girl. We don't want to get stuck out in this."

Hester twitched an ear in Rebecca's direction and picked up her pace just a little. The melt from the Chinook winds over the last couple of days had frozen now, and already patches of black ice had formed on the road. It would be particularly bad at the bridge where the highway dipped down to cross the Siksika River. It was always cool down there, which was *gut* on a hot August day, but a little scary when you had to get a horse across it without it losing its footing on the icy surface.

Just at the top of the slope on this side was the intersection with the county highway. Where Sara's parents had been killed. Where every time she passed, Rebecca thought of it. She knew Sara did, too. Rebecca could only pray that time and love would soften the edges of that jagged memory.

The countryside seemed to have gone quiet, the way it often did when it began to snow. Taking a deep breath before it was buried again. In the distance, she heard an engine. An *Englisch* car, coming fast behind her and Hester, heading for the intersection. Did people never learn? There were big yellow signs warning a *T* intersection was ahead, and the county had even installed a flashing yellow light there.

It wasn't dark yet, but Rebecca had the buggy's battery-powered lamps on just in case. Her shoulders tensed under her wool coat, and her gloved hands took a fresh grip on the reins.

"Easy, girl," she said to the horse. "It's just a big noise. It won't hurt you."

She hoped.

The car roared up behind the buggy in a blare of loud music. The driver laid on the horn and poor Hester threw up her head and juked to the right.

"Hester, *neh!*" Rebecca cried.

When she got control of the horse, up ahead she saw the car hit a patch of black ice and do a perfect three-sixty in the middle of the intersection. The driver gunned the engine to bring it out of the spin in a whirlwind of flying snow illuminated by red and yellow lights. The passenger side door opened and the music blared again as something big and black flew out of it. The car spun one more revolution while whatever it was landed hard and rolled into the shallow ravine where the river ran. A second later she heard the ice crack as something heavy hit it.

They'd lost their luggage! Or their dog! Surely now they'd stop. Surely they'd go and get whatever it was and thank their lucky stars they hadn't gone into the river, too.

She heard a female voice screaming something horrible—Rebecca would have covered her ears if her hands hadn't been clamped on the reins like claws—and the engine roared as the driver stomped on the gas pedal.

The flashy car fishtailed into a right turn on the highway, got a grip on some dry pavement, and shot forward into the dip for the bridge. In a second it was across and roaring up the other side. Rebecca had one last glimpse of red taillights from where she waited, frozen in horror, before they disappeared and the car was gone.

Hester didn't move, either, as though she wasn't quite certain it was safe yet.

Rebecca took a deep breath of air that practically crystallized her lungs. The temperature was dropping fast. "We have to get home, girl. Only a mile now."

But something laid hold of her heart and wouldn't let go.

"That big black thing that flew out—you don't suppose they really dumped their dog, do you? It won't survive the night. How can people be so cruel?"

Hester whickered, agreeing that it was often difficult to know.

"We'd better go look. I heard something hit the ice. If it's hurt, then at least we can take it home and see what Dat can do for it."

Hester nodded, and the buggy lurched into motion. Rebecca guided her to the place near the road where she'd seen the black thing go over.

"If it's only a bag of garbage or a suitcase, I'm going to be really embarrassed," she told the horse. "You wait here while I take a look."

She would have given a lot to have Joshua in the buggy with her. Twilight was gathering and she didn't even have a flashlight. But what if it was a dog down here, hurt and slowly freezing to death? The story of how Mamm and Dat had saved their dog Reggie from a similar fate back when they were young had become part of the way they'd been raised to care for animals. Every creature on the ranch had a job to do, even the cats and the chickens. Every creature was respected and looked after because, as Dat said, if you took in the innocent and expected it to do a job, you took on the responsibility of caring for it.

She'd heard something hit the ice. So she scanned the frozen margins of the river. The water was running clear in the middle, but the edges were still frozen, with rounded rocks sticking up through the cloudy ice.

There.

She scrambled closer.

And then sucked in a breath of shock so hard she coughed. Because it wasn't a dog lying half on the bank, half on the broken ice, water lapping in its hair.

It was a man.

"Ach, mein Gott, hilfe mich!"

Even to herself, Rebecca's voice sounded like a groan of horror, not a prayer for God's help. Could she go get her brothers from the ranch? *Neh*—he'd have frozen by the time they got back. She had only a few minutes to act before the cold got him.

Or had it already?

It was almost dark now, and she could barely see. She pulled off her glove and stuck a cold finger under his warm jaw, finding the spot by feel alone.

A pulse!

"Denkes, mei Vater," she breathed to her Father in heaven.

The smell of alcohol should have told her he was breathing —or maybe it was in his clothes. Well, if he was pickled, then maybe he wouldn't feel a thing when she dragged him out of here.

She picked up his legs, one foot under each arm. He was heavy, but not as heavy as a calf that didn't want to be tagged and branded in the spring. Still, it was all she could do to drag him out of the water and then, one nearly impossible heave at a time, up the shallow slope to the road where Hester waited. He was one solid individual, she'd say that for him, even if he was drunk as a skunk. His jeans were damp from snow, but thankfully he wore one of those puffy ski jackets made of nylon, which allowed him to slide behind her more easily, his arms dragging limply above his head.

All right. Into the back of the buggy. Luckily she hadn't brought the two-seater. "If you have any broken bones or a cracked skull, I'm sorry," she murmured as she somehow heaved his limp body into the back, piece by piece and limb by limb.

She jogged around to the driver's side and scrambled up. "Come on, Hester. We're going to the fire station. It's closer."

Dat might have been able to care for the dog she'd thought was in the river bottom, but the EMTs at the fire station were far better equipped to look after people. Especially *Englisch* people. She'd leave him in their capable hands and her duty to her fellow man would be concluded. But what a story she'd have to tell them all over supper!

Hester made the left turn at the intersection with only the smallest slip and clatter of her hooves. By the time Rebecca's heart had stopped pounding with fright and exertion, they had reached the fire station. She leaped out of the buggy and pounded on the door.

"Help! I need help!"

The fire captain, two volunteer firefighters, and an EMT spilled outside, pulling on their parkas with Siksika Fire on the back. While she gabbled the story of what had happened, they got him out of the buggy and strapped to a backboard, then loaded on to a gurney.

Her babbling stopped on a gasp as the station lights struck his face for the first time.

"Miss Miller?" the fire captain said. "What is it? Do you know this man?"

How to answer that? Because the truth was, she didn't.

"Vitals are low and he's unresponsive," the EMT said. "We've got to get him warmed up and down to the county hospital. Now. Any ID?"

"Not that we found," one of the firemen said.

"I know his name," Rebecca said through stiff lips.

"Good. You can go with him and tell them at County." The EMT motioned impatiently. "Come on, girl. Get in!"

The EMT boosted her into the back of the van, where the volunteer firefighter had already started the engine. The lights came on, revolving blue and red. The EMT leaped in after her and began to strap his patient down. "What's his name?"

The siren began to scream as they rolled out of the firehouse and on to the highway.

"Andrew," Rebecca croaked. "Andrew King. From Amity, Colorado."

CHAPTER 2

*T*he next two hours were a nightmare in which everyone but Rebecca knew what they were doing. She answered the EMT's questions as best she could—no, she had no idea what he was doing here. No, she didn't know what he'd been drinking. No, she didn't know who had been with him in the car or what kind of car it was, and no, she hadn't seen the driver. It might have been a female, or maybe a young man so enraged his voice had been a screech.

At the hospital, a team of people met them at the emergency bay and there didn't seem to be any option but to jog inside after them. Not unless she wanted to huddle by herself in the empty EMT van, which she really didn't. She was having second thoughts about having gone along in the first place. Poor Hester, left standing in the parking lot in the cold. Oh, Dat would be so angry. And Mamm would be worried sick, not knowing why she hadn't come home with Joshua and Sara. Maybe they'd be out looking for her already. The last thing Mamm needed was to be out in the cold with the baby due any second. But nothing would keep her inside if she thought something had happened to one of her children.

Rebecca groaned and leaned on the wall next to the closed door. Authorized Personnel Only. A person with a clipboard had stopped her here to ask a hundred more questions and escorted her here to the other side of the doors when she only knew the answers to about five.

"Miss?" A nurse in pale green scrubs offered her a cup of milky tea. "It's mint. It will help. Come on over here, to the waiting room, while they see what's what."

Rebecca sipped the tea as she followed her. The waiting room was more like a widening of the intersection of two hallways, but at least there were chairs, and low tables with magazines on them. The nurse settled on the edge of the sofa facing her.

"Are you with the patient? Andrew King?"

"Yes," she said. That much was true, she supposed. "I came in the EMT van with him."

"And your name?"

"I'm Rebecca Miller. My family's on the Circle M Ranch."

The nurse nodded. "My dad is a cattle inspector. He knows your folks."

This tiny thread of connection gave Rebecca more comfort than it probably should have. Then again, she'd never been in a hospital before. It was too far away to get to under normal circumstances, to visit people and take them flowers. And she wouldn't be coming when Mamm had the baby, either. Dat would stay here in town and bring Mamm home once the doctor said it was all right.

"And what is your relationship to Mr. King, Rebecca?"

Relationship! Oh dear, she couldn't laugh. The nurse

wouldn't understand. And she couldn't very well say she'd found him on the side of the road—that might get him in trouble. He obviously hadn't been wearing a seatbelt in that car, and he was really drunk, and both were against the law, weren't they?

"My relationship…"

"Yes," the nurse prompted.

Rebecca shook her head, and gave an embarrassed little smile. "All I've wanted since last summer was to be his wife. But that's not going to happen, is it?"

The nurse put a comforting hand on Rebecca's wrist. "Oh, honey, don't lose heart. Dr. Goldstein is on duty in the ER tonight, and he's really good. So far they've determined Andrew has a dislocated shoulder, a fractured tibia, and a touch of hypothermia. We'll get those fixed as soon as he's stable."

"Stable?"

"Yes. They're afraid of an injury to the brain. Do you know what happened?"

How could she know? He'd been hundreds of miles from home, in an *Englisch* car, drunk, and probably with an *Englisch* girl, who had left him to freeze to death. How was she going to say all that to this nice nurse with the big, sympathetic eyes?

"I don't know," she said at last. "It was dark, and he fell out of a car, and when I reached him, he was half in the river and not conscious. So I got him into the buggy and took him to the fire station. And the EMT van brought us here."

The nurse sat back, her eyes glowing. "You saved his life. You know that, right?"

Rebecca looked down at her hands, twisting in the fabric

of her old taupe work dress. "God did. I just happened to be there."

"That's so romantic, saving your fiancé's life." The nurse clasped both hands over her heart. "What a story you're going to have to tell your kids."

"Oh, but he's not—"

An alarm sounded and the red light by the door began to flash.

"Oh my. Another one coming in. This freeze is going to play merry havoc with the roads tonight. People will just never learn to slow down." The nurse jumped up. "You just stay right there, honey. As soon as I know whether he's going on to the ward or into ICU, I'll come and get you."

But she didn't. Hours went by and the waiting room slowly filled up. By ten o'clock, the ice on the highway had claimed two cars and an empty school bus. Rebecca fell asleep in her chair with the vague feeling that she ought to find a telephone and call the cell phone that resided in the cookie jar at home.

Sometime toward morning, the nurse came back and woke her.

"He's in the ICU now, honey," she said. "Normally we wouldn't allow anyone in until he regains consciousness, but you're the next thing to family, aren't you?" She twinkled at Rebecca, whose brain felt like it was made of quilt batting. "You come along with me. I want you to be the first thing he sees when he wakes up."

What a horrible thought. Rebecca Miller, a girl he never noticed or even saw when she was in Amity last summer. Now here she was, her hair half falling down, and her mouth tasting like one of her brothers' socks.

The nurse let her use the bathroom on the ward, and wash her face and do her best to repair her hair and smooth it under her bucket-shaped *Kapp*. She'd managed to lose one of the three straight pins that held it on. Hopefully two would still do the job. Her away bonnet had got mud on it somehow, so she tied the strings and looped it over her arm.

She was ushered into a long, L-shaped room divided by glass partitions, some containing people, some not. An old lady muttered and twitched in the one nearest the door, and two elderly men struggled to breathe under plastic masks in the next two. In the second room from the end lay a still figure.

"We've given him a bath and put the shoulder back in," the nurse said. "Don't be alarmed by the bruises. Those are from the fall."

Rebecca could see one on his cheekbone. How many of them had been from her bumping him up the slope to the buggy and heaving him in? How had she even done that? He had to outweigh her by sixty or seventy pounds.

And then her whole being seemed to be consumed by that face—the one she'd touched a hundred times in her dreams. With the firm chin and the mouth made for kissing. Oh my, he'd had his hair cut in the *Englisch* style. At least he smelled a little less like a distillery.

"Is he drunk still?" she whispered to the nurse.

"It probably saved him from serious hypothermia," she said practically. "His blood alcohol level was one point zero. What were you two were doing out there?"

"Going home." At least she was. "One point zero—is that bad?"

"The legal limit is point zero eight."

Oh. That was bad.

"He wasn't driving, was he?" the nurse asked.

"No."

"Were you?"

Rebecca shook her head. "Just the buggy. Oh—my horse! I left poor Hester at the fire station. Do you think someone took care of her?"

The nurse patted her arm. "I'll go check. Meanwhile, you sit right here and talk to him. We've induced a coma, considering his brain is a bit swollen."

"Can he hear me?" She'd never seen anyone in any kind of coma before. He just looked as if he were asleep. And if he was like Malena, he wouldn't hear a thing. Her twin slept so deeply that Adam and Zach had once rolled her onto the floor as a prank, and she'd spent the whole night on the braided rug without knowing the difference.

"There's some evidence to say a person under sedation like this can hear us," the nurse said, already on her way to the door. "Does he have any family besides you who ought to know? If so, feel free to use the phone there, next to the bed."

Rebecca sank into the chair between the bed and the window, and gazed at the phone with something akin to horror. She hated the phone. The tinny sound of people's voices, the way she couldn't see their faces. But she had to call home. And Andrew's home, too.

He lived with his brothers. Or he had. Had he left his family and the carpentry business? Had something gone horribly wrong since last summer to make him plunge into the *Englisch* world with a vengeance? While they might have a cell phone for emergencies, she certainly didn't know the number. She could call Information and get the number for

King Cuts and Meats, maybe. Tell Joshua, Amanda's husband.

Yes, that's what she'd do. She'd figure out how. In a minute. Once she got done memorizing his face, now that she was no longer on the far side of some room, invisible. Now that she was close enough to—

Hardly able to believe she could be so daring, she reached out and touched his hair with one finger, lifting it gently out of his eyes. When he didn't even twitch an eyelid, she plucked up her courage and laid her whole hand against his strong, angled jaw, just the way she had in all her dreams.

His skin was so warm—much warmer than she expected, considering he'd come within a whisker of freezing to death. As though his temperature—or her own nerve—had burned her, she pulled her hand back and clasped it in her lap.

She had to let her family know where she was.

She must call the Kings and tell them Andrew was in a coma and no one knew when he might wake up.

She ought to straighten out the misunderstanding she'd already let go on too long, and tell the nurse she wasn't actually engaged to him.

And she would. Just as soon as she slaked the thirst of months and months, and got enough of drinking in the sight of him. Here, where she could.

Where no one would ever know.

Including him.

His arms lay outside the covers. On the far side, a needle was taped into the crook of his elbow, another in the back of his hand, hooked to the apparatus from which bags of clear liquid hung. But on this side, his hand lay on the blanket.

She took it in hers. How strange it felt to hold this man's

hand. She'd held hands with boys, of course, on a date or two. Not many. Kissed one of them, even. She'd never get a reputation for being fast at that rate. But their hands had been clammy, or cold, or rough with calluses from ranch work. Andrew's wasn't really rough, though he was a carpenter. But it felt like a man's hand. Larger than her own. Capable, somehow. Not like those boys' hands.

Her fingers slid between his.

"I don't know if you can hear me," she whispered. Well, no one could hear her if she didn't speak up. Hadn't Mamm said that a million times? "But if you *can* hear me, my name is Rebecca Miller. We're in the county hospital in Libby, Montana. You've got some swelling on the brain, so that's why they've made you sleep."

He didn't respond. His chest just rose and fell, rose and fell.

"I hope you don't mind that I'm holding your hand. You see, if I were you, I'd want to know someone was with me. I'd want my family with me. But if you're here and not in Amity, I don't know what happened. Did you have a fight with your brothers? You sure must have had a fight with that *Englisch* girl for her to dump you out of the car and leave you there. I hope you pick your friends more carefully next time."

No response.

The monitors beeped like sleepy chicks. It was warm in here. She should take off her black wool coat. She was getting pretty sleepy, too.

"Can I tell you a secret?" She yawned. "I've been in love with you for almost a year. Dreaming of the day when you'd turn and give me that wonderful smile."

She'd lay her head down here on the side of the bed for a second. Right by his hand.

She pressed his palm to her face, the way he had a thousand times in her dreams. "And then you'd ask me to marry you," she mumbled into the blanket. "And I'd say yes."

She didn't see the nurse at the door, or the way she smiled.

By the time the nurse tiptoed over to check the monitors, Rebecca was sound asleep.

CHAPTER 3

*N*oah King woke with a jolt as the *Englisch* taxi van rocked to a halt. He rubbed his eyes and peered out the side window, trying not to disturb his sleeping mother, whose head lay on his shoulder. For a moment, he was disoriented. The sun was about an hour over the mountains. But the mountains were on the wrong side. Was it after sunrise? Or nearly sunset?

"Where are we?" His voice came out like a croak and startled Jimmy, their *Englisch* driver.

"Welcome to Mountain Home, Montana," Jimmy said like a radio announcer, waking up both his wife, Darlene, in the passenger seat and Mamm, who straightened and gazed around her with a frightened look on her face.

"We're here, Mamm," he said. "Amity to Mountain Home in twenty hours flat."

"It feels like it, too," she said. "Can we get out?"

"Looks like the Bitterroot Dutch Café is open," Jimmy said. "We could grab a bite before we go out to your new home, or just go straight there. Up to you."

19

Dat gazed out the window and looked at Mamm. "Not as flat here on this side of the Rockies. Wonder if the growing season is as short?"

Which didn't really help with the decision.

Simeon, the eldest, took matters in hand, as he tended to do. "We'll have some breakfast here. What are the odds Andrew stocked the fridge at the new place, and has breakfast ready?"

"Slim to none. Let's eat!" Their sisters Clara and Patricia hauled on the sliding door of the van and spilled out. Their parents followed, and Jimmy and Darlene, and by the time they filled three tables inside, the little café was nearly at capacity.

The proprietor, an Amish woman, looked delighted at their crowd. "Well now, it's nice to see Amish folks out and about on a holiday, even if it is a little early in the year." She handed out menus. "Where are you all from?"

"Kentucky," Dat said. "Arlon and Kate King. Our sons, Simeon and Noah. Our daughters, Clara and Patricia."

Her eyebrows rose. "Kentucky, hey? That's a fair distance. Nice to meet you all. Coffee?"

Noah barely restrained himself from offering up his mug like Oliver Twist. "My brothers and I have been in Amity, in Colorado. But my folks decided to move up here."

"I'm Ellie Bontrager. My daughter Susan and I bought this café just a couple of months ago, when my boys took over the ranch. Have to keep busy, don't we?" She poured coffee with the expertise of a woman with a large family. "We heard you all were coming to Annie Gingerich's place."

"She's my aunt," Mamm said. "She'll be moving back into

the big house with us from the *Daadi Haus,* once we get it fixed up."

"That house has been standing empty for years," Ellie said, lowering the empty pot. "It's pretty run down."

"That's why we've come along," Simeon said. "My brothers and I are carpenters. We have a business in Amity."

A business that Sim was good at, in a town that he liked, with family close by. And then they'd crossed the state line into Montana yesterday, just at sunset, and Noah had thrown all his life's plans into disarray by falling in love.

With the mountains. The big skies. The sheer scale of it.

Montana didn't look a bit like Colorado. It was said to be the land of wide open spaces, and it was, on the east side. But northwest Montana had its own wild beauty and it had captured Noah, heart and soul.

Noah had gone into carpentry with Sim because he hadn't really found any other work that satisfied him. Building homes for people and barns for animals was satisfying, as far as it went. And yet he'd been more anxious to get to Aendi Annie's ranch than anything he could remember. Their unfamiliarity with ranch life gave his father deep misgivings, but they'd committed themselves because Mamm had lived here with her aunt and uncle as a child, and there was a deep bond between them still. But to Noah, working a ranch sounded like exactly what he wanted to do. As though it would satisfy some need deep inside him. To create a home not for a paying customer, but for himself. To bring about change, and yet belong.

A need that Simeon wouldn't understand at all. He preferred to belong where things didn't change much, and when they did, he controlled exactly how much.

Sim, as Clara never tired of reminding him, was a stick in the mud. A likeable, dependable one, but still.

"And then we'll see what can be done with the ranch," Mamm was saying. "I'll have the waffles with eggs and sausage, please."

"We'll get it running again," Dat said. "The Hungry Rancher Platter."

"You've got a row to hoe there," Ellie told him, writing rapidly. "The folks at the Double Diamond leased it for grazing and did some upkeep, but not all."

"I've hoed plenty of rows," Dat said.

When the food came out, and after their silent grace, Noah found it hot and homemade and excellent. Ellie was bound to have a roaring trade in her new venture.

Patricia said to their hostess, "Have you met our brother Andrew? He's been getting the house livable for us."

Ellie poured a second round of coffee while she thought.

Noah felt a tingle of alarm. That was way too much thinking for such a simple question.

"Can't say I have," she said at last. "How long has he been here?"

"A month at least," Sim told her, chewing more slowly now that the implications were setting in.

"He hasn't been to church?" Dat said. "Hasn't Annie introduced him to the bishop?"

"Not that I know of," Ellie said slowly. "But then, we've been pretty busy getting the restaurant organized and open for business. Susan!" she hollered into the kitchen. "Come on out for a second, will you?"

A young woman bustled out, and her mother introduced them all. Her gaze lingered on Noah and Sim, and he felt himself being sized up and catalogued as husband material before she even spoke.

"Have you met Andrew King at any of the jamborees with the *Youngie* lately?" Ellie asked her. "He's supposed to have been getting Annie Gingerich's farmhouse ready."

Susan shook her head. "Maybe he has been, but if so, he hasn't been off the place. There's been no one new in town since Sara Fischer came back at Christmas. Though I suppose she's not really new. She was born and raised here."

"That's not right," Dat muttered.

"I knew I shouldn't have let him get on that bus," Sim said with a groan. "I don't know what's got into him."

"I do," Dat said grimly. "The world, that's what. He's left the Amish way twice already. I thought he liked working with you in Amity. I thought he would stay this time."

"I did, too," Sim said.

Noah had the wild urge to slide under the table before both his elder brother and his father pinned him in place with their gazes. "Did you know he was going to throw over the traces and bolt?" Dat demanded. "Again?"

That tone—that one right there—was the one that made their brother Andrew a little crazy. He'd been on the receiving end of it far more often than Noah and Sim ever had, and had never built up an immunity to it. It made him feel just as bad every time. Just as rebellious. Just as angry.

"Do you think he would tell me?" Noah said as mildly as he could. "I haven't heard a word since he left. I thought the same as you—that he was here, working on the house."

"So much for trusting him," Sim said. "He probably went to Missouri or something instead."

"Of course you should trust your brother," Mamm told

him, tears starting in her eyes. "He's a *gut sohn*. He's just having a hard time right now. Trying to decide who his friends are. He's—"

"In love," Clara said. Then her eyes went wide as her entire family turned to stare at her.

Jimmy and Darlene, at the next table, spoke in low voices to each other, completely unconscious of the crisis happening in their midst. Susan and Ellie stood transfixed, as though everyone but Noah had forgotten they were there.

Which was probably true.

"What did you say?" Dat said in a tone he probably thought was gentle, but which Clara clearly did not. She turned pale.

"Clara?" Mamm said. "Do you know something we don't?"

"N-not really," Clara stammered. "It's just something Amanda said when we were at their place last Sunday. That he had a girlfriend. But maybe it was just a rumor. He didn't confide in her or anything."

"He didn't tell me, either," Sim said, sounding aggrieved. "I don't know anything about any girlfriend, and I lived with the man."

Noah had an *aha!* moment. "How did he get up here?" he asked his family. "Anybody know?"

"By bus, how else?" Sim said. "I thought he'd get on the train later. Amtrak goes through Colorado and stops in Libby."

"However he got here, he's been skylarking around while we thought he was working on the house." Dat's voice was back to being grim. He took Mamm's hand under the table. *"Fraa,* you'd best prepare yourself."

"But why didn't Aendi Annie say anything?" Mamm said,

at a loss. "I've had two letters from her in the last month and she didn't mention a thing about his not being here."

But that was a question none of them could answer.

Dat released her hand and mopped up the last of his egg yolk and sausage gravy with half a biscuit. "I guess we'll find out soon enough. Ellie, could we get some of that excellent coffee to go? And Jimmy, maybe you wouldn't mind stopping at the grocery store so we can pick up a few things. I have a feeling there isn't exactly a homecoming feast prepared for us."

FROM FAMILY LORE, Noah had long known that Annie and Albert Gingerich had been one of the first to settle in the Siksika Lake region. Fifty or sixty years ago, families had trickled in to find pasture and ranch land cheap, and the profits from the beef industry enough to live on. The town of Mountain Home, once not much more than a bar and a gas station, now boasted a couple dozen businesses, many of them owned and operated by descendants of those original families.

Annie had hung on to the Gingerich ranch even as she saw her own sons and daughters move away or be called home to the Lord. She leased its acres and its grazing allotment to the Rocking Diamond, which had given her enough to live on. But now, as Noah got out of the van and took in the house, he realized that while Annie herself had been under the watchful care of the church district, the old house had not.

"She couldn't keep it up," Mamm said, sounding almost apologetic. "She rented it out to a string of folks, but if you're renting, you're not going to put as much care into a place as if it were your own."

"No," he agreed. "Sim and I will go over it and see what it needs. If you're going to live here and take care of Aendi Annie, we want to be certain you're comfortable."

"And hold church here again," she said. "Annie's looking forward to that."

The house had been big and welcoming once. It was still big, but it needed a lot before it was welcoming once more. Like paint. And no doubt some structural work on the inside. Dual-pane windows. That wraparound porch begged for visitors on summer evenings, but it sagged in the middle, telling him that the support beams had likely rotted.

The front door of the *Daadi Haus*, sitting next to a vast rectangular garden of dead vegetable stalks and dormant raspberry canes, opened, and a tiny, bent figure appeared on the porch.

"Aendi Annie!" Mamm called, and the family fell in behind her as she hurried over. Behind them, Jimmy began to unload the suitcases from the back of the van.

But Annie did not look as though the sight of them was the best gift she'd had all day.

"Annie, what's the matter?" Mamm slipped an arm around her. "Come inside. It's too cold to be standing out here, shawl or no shawl."

They filled the living room to capacity as they dropped into the sofa and the chairs. The house smelled of bacon and furniture polish and was immaculately clean. Noah remained standing. Listening as his elderly great-aunt spoke, the wrinkles in her soft cheeks creasing even deeper with distress.

"I have a cell phone. For emergencies, like most of the

families here. Hardly ever works, but this time it did. Just past sunup I got a call from Reuben Miller, over on the Circle M," she said. "One of the volunteer firemen called them last night to say their girl Rebecca had gone down to Libby in the ambulance and would they come and get the horse."

"Is she all right?" Dat asked, since Annie had paused and someone needed to say something. None of them knew the Millers, but still, an ambulance was serious.

"Oh, she's fine. But that's not the point. Reuben's call was to tell me who else was in the ambulance. Their boy Adam found out when he got to the fire station for his shift. He's training to be an EMT."

"Found out what?" Dat asked patiently.

"It was your *Andrew*," Aendi Annie said, as though she'd been trying to tell him and he kept interrupting.

"What?" Dat's eyes widened in horror.

"He's in a bad way from some kind of accident. The Millers knew you all were coming, so that's why they called so early, to see if I'd heard from you. I've been on tenterhooks all morning."

Maybe they shouldn't have stopped for those groceries after all, Noah thought. Andrew in hospital? What had happened? How bad was *in a bad way*?

Mamm made a motion with her hands as though she was clearing a path through a thicket. "Annie, I don't understand. Andrew has been here, hasn't he? For the last month? Working on the house?"

The old woman looked confused. *"Neh.* I haven't seen hide nor hair of him. But what are you waiting for, Kate? You and Arlon have to go down to Libby right away. He's in a coma, and nobody knows whether he's going to live or die."

At which point Noah learned something about Aendi Annie's tendency to deliver news, good or bad. A long buildup, and then the crash.

Mamm collapsed in tears. So did his sisters.

Noah went outside to ask Jimmy and Darlene if they'd put a few more gallons of gas in the van and take the family back to Libby. Simeon gave all their groceries to Aendi Annie and said they'd call as soon as they had news.

And ten minutes later the whole family was back on the highway, heading south.

CHAPTER 4

*R*ebecca swam up through the dark depths of sleep, pulled to the surface by the sound of whispering. *Deitsch* whispering, like waves on a shore. Such a comforting sound, after all the *Englisch* voices, some harsh, some kind, all around her since last night. Or was it the night before? What day was it?

"Is that her?"

"Of course it's her, Mamm."

"The one who came in the ambulance with him."

"Oh, look! Her cheek is resting on his hand."

"That's so sweet."

"It must be true, what the nurse said."

"This is the girlfriend?"

"Shh! She's waking up."

Rebecca opened her eyes to find her face cradled in Andrew's warm but unresponsive hand. She'd drooled on his fingers. With the wrist of her dress, she rubbed them dry and swiped at her cheek, which probably had his handprint pressed into it. Her *Kapp* was askew, but it wasn't until she turned to look for the second straight pin—*oh, please don't let it have fallen in his blankets, just waiting to stick him*—that she saw the anxious crowd of people at the end of the bed.

With a gasp, she reared back and clocked her head on a piece of medical equipment.

"Oh, you poor thing!" said a teenage girl of maybe fifteen.

"We didn't mean to scare you, honest," said a second one, a couple of years older.

"We've heard all about you," said a woman who had to be Andrew's mother, if those eyes were any indication. "How you came in the ambulance, and have been here by his side all this time."

"You are Rebecca Miller?" a man asked. Oldest son, probably. The serious, take-charge type, like her brother Daniel.

"Ja," she finally rasped, and massaged the back of her head. Last night's glass of water still sat on Andrew's bed table where she'd left it. She gulped it down. "Are you his relatives?" They must be. They wouldn't let anyone in here who wasn't family.

Except her. Which they'd find out soon enough, and boot her out of the hospital to find her own way home.

"Ja," said the man who must be his father. He made the introductions. Arlon and Kate King. Simeon, Noah, Patricia, and Clara, the youngest.

"We have two married sisters, too," Patricia said helpfully. "But they didn't come with us."

Come with them where? Here? From Colorado? But the trio of carpenters had no parents living with them, unless something had changed. She was so confused. Maybe she should ask that nice nurse to look at her head when she came back.

"How is he?" Kate moved to the other side of the bed, and Rebecca remembered her manners.

"Please. Have the chair," she said, standing awkwardly, feeling all arms and legs.

"No, dear. I've been sitting in the van for twenty hours straight. More. You stay right there." She looked down at her son, her eyes full of tears. She looked as heartbroken as if he had died. "Andrew, *mei sohn*, what happened to you?"

"The nurse told us, Mamm," the younger son said. Noah. "The ice was bad. There was an accident. He was thrown from a car. This young woman took him to the fire station."

Noah looked familiar. Of course he did. They'd met in Colorado. Then again, it had been almost a year, and anyway, people tended to not remember her.

As he met her gaze, recognition sparked in those dark eyes that looked so much like Andrew's and their mother's.

She was more surprised than he was.

If she were being honest, she could have passed him on the street and felt only a vague sense of having seen him before. Because all her earthly being had been focused on Andrew for all those months. Amity might as well have been a ghost town for all the attention she paid to any other living person. Except Amanda and Joshua King, her hosts.

"So you really did save his life." Kate's voice trembled.

"*Neh, der Herr* saved it," Rebecca said once again. "I was just His instrument."

"Oh, I'm so happy *der Herr* directed you there just in time." Patricia flung her arms around Rebecca, who instinctively hugged her back.

"And you're engaged!" Clara said. "I never thought I'd see

the day, but I'm so glad you are!" And then she hugged her, too.

"Well, I—" she said, trying to surface from their enthusiastic embraces.

"Goodness sakes, girls, let the poor young woman breathe," Arlon said. "She's been through a harrowing night and spent half of it watching over Andrew. She's probably only had two hours' sleep."

"But I want to hear all about it," Patricia said.

"We don't need to hear this very minute," Kate told her daughter, then beamed at Rebecca. "But oh, I'm so happy it's you." She came around the bed and Rebecca was again engulfed in a hug. And she'd thought *her* family was affectionate. "For a while he was tangled up with some *Englisch* girl, and we were so afraid he might go back to her—"

"Mamm, I'm sure she doesn't want to hear about some *Englisch* girl," Simeon said.

"But now he has an Amish sweetheart, just as I've always hoped!" Kate pressed her cheek to Rebecca's, and she felt the dampness of tears. "You'll be his salvation, and I can only thank *der gut Gott* for it."

His salvation? She really had to put a stop to this. Rebecca opened her mouth, marshaling the right words.

"Excuse me, folks, but the twenty minutes are up." A different nurse from the one who had been so nice last night was standing in the doorway. This one didn't look quite so nice. "You, too, Miss Miller. We need to give Mr King a bath and then the neurologist is going to examine him. You can come back in at two o'clock. He should be ready for visitors by then."

"You come with us," Arlon said to her. "You're family now. We'll go have lunch."

"We just had breakfast," Noah objected.

"That was forty miles ago," Clara informed him. "Besides, I bet Rebecca hasn't had breakfast."

She couldn't remember when her last meal had been. *"Neh*, I—"

"There, you see?" Clara tilted her chin at her brother. "Don't be so selfish, Noah."

"Don't call your brother names, Clara," their mother said, as though they were all six years old. "Come along, everyone, and Rebecca can tell us all about her courtship with Andrew. I can't think of anything that would give me more joy. And believe me, after all this, I can use some joy."

And Rebecca was carried away by the King family, everyone one of whom wanted to hear what she had to say.

Maybe it was a sin, but the feeling of being the center of attention was so novel, so outside of normal experience, that she couldn't help but enjoy it. She knew perfectly well that if allowing it was a sin, then enjoying it was even more so. And she would be punished for it.

But just for a few minutes, it couldn't do any harm.

When they sat down to lunch, for sure and certain she'd tell them the truth.

❧

NAOMI MILLER HAD FORGOTTEN ALL the aches and pains that came with being heavily pregnant. Or maybe it was the aches and pains that came from being pregnant at the age of forty-nine that made them seem new. She couldn't seem to get comfortable—no matter how she sat or stood, her joints and ligaments protested. Her enormous belly was a horizon over which she couldn't see, and the pains of early labor had been coming and going since this morning.

"Are you all right, *Liewi?*" Reuben's voice held a tinge of anxiety, which meant his heart was probably overflowing with it.

She touched his cheek, her fingers warm from the mug of herbal tea Sara had made instead of afternoon coffee. It smelled like summer, from Sarah Byler's herb box recently arrived from Whinburg Township. Their Sara was learning to be a *Dokterfraa*, and while Naomi was no judge, the tea seemed to help with the heartburn and sometimes even the emotions that went with this stage.

"I'm well," she said softly to her husband. "It's begun, but the hard part is a ways off yet. I wish it were over already—I want to cuddle our little Deborah."

His smile told her that she'd succeeded in making him feel less anxious.

"Mind you," she went on, "I'd like to cuddle my Rebecca, too. Does anybody know when she's coming home? What's keeping her, down there in the hospital?"

"It hasn't even been twelve hours, Mamm." Joshua, with baby Nathan in his lap, helped himself to another of the chocolate chip cookies on the plate. "Of all times to have a car, though, this would have been a good one. We could have gone and fetched her."

"That would be the end of our baptism classes," his fiancée Sara reminded him, wrapping her thin hands around her own mug of tea and leaning on his shoulder. "Adam says the EMTs run down to the hospital all the time. He'll go down with the next one, and bring Rebecca back with him."

Well, that was something. "But what about this King boy?" Naomi said. "I didn't know she even knew him, never mind well enough to go in the ambulance all the way to Libby. Why didn't she just come home in the buggy?"

But these were questions her family couldn't answer. Even Adam hadn't known her reasons, only that she knew the identity of the victim, and in the chaos of thinking he might die unidentified, they had bundled her in. If only Adam had been on shift, such a thing would never have happened.

But *if only* was just a story people told themselves. *If only* never helped.

Suddenly restless, Naomi finished the rest of her tea and got up. It wasn't right, that her girl—so shy, so quiet—should be tossed into an unheard-of situation without her family to help her. Did she have any money? Where was she getting food?

Another pain came. Her body was getting down to business.

"Reuben, I think we should call Liam."

Liam Kennedy, one of the other apprentices at John Cooper's saddlery, had become friendly with Joshua and had promised to take her and Reuben to the hospital in his truck.

Sara put down her mug. "Naomi? Is it time?"

Reuben already had the cell phone in his hand. After six children, he knew what to do, even though the last one had been more than twenty years ago.

"Ja," she said, a little breathlessly. "Sara, my bag is in the mud room. Joshua, I know you still have that phone. Call the

doctor—her number is on the card right on top. She told us to come down early, not to wait."

While a younger woman living closer to the hospital might not go in until her contractions came every five minutes, Naomi knew her situation was different. She didn't feel "high risk," but all the same, she was glad Dr Gupta was taking every precaution.

The *Youngie* scattered to do her bidding while she stood at the end of the kitchen table, hanging on to it and watching the minute hand sweep around the clock until Reuben could help her into the bedroom to put her shoes on.

"You'll be all right," he said, his warm fingers cradling her stocking-clad foot. "We're old hands at this." She knew he meant to comfort her, but half of it was to reassure himself, poor man. Neither of them had forgotten the ordeal of the twins' birth, nor the hours of agony it had cost before they'd been rewarded with two little girls.

"Liam will be here in ten minutes," Sara reported from outside the door. "We'll look after dinner and tell the others when they come in."

It was the tail end of calving season, and the fact that Reuben was in the house at all was a miracle. Her boys were all out in the pastures, keeping an eye on the cows who were lagging behind and hadn't yet given birth.

Dr Gupta said she'd meet them at the hospital, Liam came in eight minutes, and off they went. For Naomi, the forty-mile trip was a blur of counting minutes between contractions and scenery whizzing by outside. The only thing that was crystal clear was being wheeled up to the elevator and when it opened, seeing their Rebecca standing there surrounded by a crowd of Amish people she'd never seen before.

"Mamm!" she cried. "Is the baby—"

"*Ja*," Reuben said to their daughter. "Are you going up with us?"

And then the pains really starting coming, and all Naomi could do was groan and hold on to Reuben's hand as he jogged beside her wheelchair up to the delivery room.

ॐ

REBECCA WAS ONCE AGAIN LEFT outside a pair of doors labeled Authorized Personnel Only feeling as though she'd been caught up in a tornado and set down so suddenly she didn't recognize her surroundings.

Which she didn't. The waiting room here had pictures of yellow ducklings and puppies and kittens on the walls, which the ICU waiting room downstairs certainly did not.

After a minute or two, when the door didn't open by itself, she turned and practically ran into Noah King's chest. "Oh!"

He steadied her and peered into her face. "Is everything all right? I thought you were going with your mother."

"I was. But only one person is allowed in the delivery room. My father went with her."

"Why did they have you go with them?"

"Because I disappeared in the middle of the night and they're my parents?" She frowned at him. "Though Dat probably wouldn't have let me go in anyway. I've seen plenty of pregnant women, but never been in a delivery room. He's got more experience."

He almost smiled.

"What are you doing up here?"

He looked a little surprised that she should ask. "There's

an *Englisch* boy downstairs. He brought your parents in. He's wondering what he's supposed to do."

"Oh. Liam Kennedy. I guess I'd better tell him it's going to be a while and he shouldn't wait."

She walked over to the elevator, and to her surprise, he got in with her. The doors closed on them and shut off the hospital noises except for the whine of the machinery. She was uncomfortably aware that she'd slept in her clothes and could probably use a good wash.

"So ... who's Liam Kennedy?" he asked, watching the lights blink down. Three. Two.

"He and my brother Joshua are apprentices to John Cooper, the saddle maker. He offered to bring Mamm here when her time came."

One. The doors opened on the lobby.

"That was kind of him."

She didn't think this observation needed a reply, and anyway, there was Liam in his range coat, turning his brown felt Stetson in his hands and looking uncomfortable.

"Rebecca," Liam said with relief. "Did she get here in time? I wasn't sure what I'd do if she had the baby in the truck."

Rebecca tried to smile, but that idea came a little too close for comfort. "Dat would have delivered my little sister like a calf," she said, turning it into a joke. "But she's nowhere near having the baby yet, so you ought to go on home."

"Are you sure?" He looked anxious, as though he meant to stay the night, just in case.

"I'm sure. Thank you so much for getting her here safely. Dat is in the delivery room, and so is her doctor, so all I need to do now is wait."

"You ought to go home with him," Noah said.

She'd forgotten he was there. "What? Why?"

"Because you spent the night with my brother and you're probably ready to be with your family."

Liam's eyebrows went up and Rebecca could have smacked Noah for putting it like that. "Maybe your parents ought to go," she suggested, trying not to sound as aggravated as she felt. "Didn't your mother say something about a twenty-hour drive? They must be exhausted."

"Do they need a ride to Mountain Home?" Liam asked. "My truck will fit five. It has the extended cab."

"We can't impose on you like that," Noah said, shaking his head.

"But what are you all going to do?" Rebecca asked him. "Andrew could wake up tonight ... or three weeks from now. His brother is in an induced coma," she explained to Liam. "The family just got here this afternoon."

"And the *Englisch* taxi has gone," Noah said. "I suppose we'll all get a motel." He paused, looking pained. "Except our suitcases are all at Aendi Annie's."

"Sounds like I'm your best option," Liam said cheerfully. "You go have a conflab with your family and figure it out. I'll hang around."

"And you still haven't had anything to eat," Noah said to Rebecca. "You never made it to the cafeteria."

Her stomach gave a great big growl as if it had been waiting to answer him. She could have sunk through the floor.

"I'll take that as agreement," Noah said. "Come on. Liam, you too. The family is all in the cafeteria. Even if they don't take you up on your offer, at least we can give you a meal as a thank you."

An hour later, Liam's truck, its extended cab full to the windows with Kings, pulled out of the hospital parking lot, leaving Rebecca and Noah waving from inside the big double glass doors that slid apart when you stood on the mat.

On the good side, her stomach was full. Mamm was in the capable hands of a doctor she trusted. Rebecca would soon have a baby sister to cuddle and love. And with the *Englisch* cowboy Liam at the table with them in the cafeteria, the subject of her engagement to Andrew and her confession that it was all a misunderstanding had not had a chance to come up.

On the bad side, now she couldn't go upstairs and sit with Andrew. Because there hadn't been room for all of the family in Liam's truck, so Noah had stayed behind.

And something about him told her that Liam or no Liam, he planned to get to the bottom of this engagement business, and there would be no getting out of a confession.

CHAPTER 5

*N*oah had never been in this position before—with a strange girl, in a strange place, in even stranger circumstances. This was where Simeon tended to shine. When you needed someone to take charge and look after people, he was your man. But here, in a hospital? Already Sim had been fidgety with the inaction, the inability to wake Andrew up, his powerlessness in an *Englisch* institution. Not that any of them were comfortable in such a place. But it was just as well Sim had understood he was needed to look after their parents and the girls. Mamm was exhausted and worried sick; the best place for her was Aendi Annie's, where there was a lot to do, not sitting in a dimly lit room watching their brother sleep, not knowing if he'd ever wake up.

Simeon was certainly itching to get a look at their home. He'd led most of the conversation over their meal in the cafeteria. Making a plan for repairs. Asking Liam Kennedy who had the best prices for building supplies. Noah could practically see the punch list forming in his brother's head, minute by minute. And that was *gut*. It was the reason they'd taken this time away from Amity—to help their parents and do what they could until the snow and bad weather gave in to the soft persuasions of spring and the building season got under way in Colorado. There was no work in the Wet Mountain Valley until the weather warmed up, and you couldn't guarantee that until May. Now was the time for their parents to make the move, and for the three King brothers to make their new home comfortable.

Well, two of the three King brothers. Noah felt a ripple of irritation at Andrew's complete lack of responsibility that had landed all of them in a situation no one could have planned for.

And that included the silent girl standing beside him in the hospital lobby.

In the cafeteria, Sim's focus had been on their home, not on finding out just exactly what Rebecca Miller was doing here with Andrew. Because something felt off to Noah. He didn't know what, but it niggled in the back of his mind like a worm on a hook.

Rebecca turned from the door with a forlorn expression, and he forgot about worms and hooks in the sudden realization that they'd all been enormously selfish.

"I'm sorry, Rebecca," he said. "I should have insisted you go home with them." Good grief. She'd been here all night—after saving Andrew's life.

"I could have insisted, too, but I didn't," she said, and then her pale face flushed with embarrassment, right up to the roots of her blond hair. "I'm sorry. That was rude."

He was sorry. Now she was sorry. Surely he could do better than this.

"You're right. There's no excuse for—"

But she shook her head. "I wanted to stay. When Mamm has the baby, I'll be the first to see her. And when Andrew wakes up—"

"Like the doctor said, it could be days before it's safe to bring him out of it. You're not going to hang around here for days, are you?"

"I've got nowhere to stay," she said after a moment, as though this were the first time it had occurred to her. "There aren't any Amish folks in town, like there are in Mountain Home. But the nurse said that even if my mother had the baby tonight, they were going to keep her for twenty-four hours, just to make sure. Because she's an older mother."

"There's nothing wrong, is there?"

Rebecca shook her head. "I don't think so. But I'm glad of it. If something goes wrong or the baby needs help, she's in the right place."

"That leaves you and your father needing a bed for the night," he said. "Me too. Come on. Why don't we arrange that?"

He might as well have said, *Why don't we arrange to sleep on the railroad tracks?* from the shocked and apprehensive look on her face.

"I—I don't— What would Dat say?"

"He would say, *thank goodness you thought of it, because they won't let me sleep in the recovery room.* Our *Englisch* driver pointed out a bed and breakfast on the way in. I think I can find it again."

"A bed and breakfast?" At least she was putting on her coat. "Wouldn't a motel be cheaper?"

"Maybe," he said. "But the motels are up on the highway, a couple of miles from here. There's more snow coming, and what if we have to get back to the hospital in a hurry? It's a long way to run."

She nodded, tying the strings of her mud-streaked away bonnet in a bow under her chin. "You're right. And I suppose as long as Mamm and little Deborah are both well, Dat won't care where he sleeps. During roundup, he sleeps in a tent, with nothing but a camping mat between him and the ground."

Would Noah himself get a chance to go on roundup? And sleep in a tent? He hoped so. He shrugged into his own coat and wedged on his felt hat, then stood on the mat to make the door open for her. They headed down the hospital driveway to the street, turned left, and he let his internal guidance system retrace the *Englisch* taxi's route.

"Roundup—that's when you bring the cows down from the summer pastures? Aendi Annie has talked about it in her letters."

"Yes. We call it *turnout* when we take the mothers and calves up the mountain in the spring. Same basic process, only in reverse and with mud."

He laughed—probably the first time he'd laughed since he woke up in the van this morning.

Had it only been this morning?

"I've been carpentering for several years now," he said, "but I'd sure like to try my hand at cowboying. I don't suppose it will happen, though. I'm in business with my brothers and we have to go back once the house is livable for my parents and sisters."

They turned a corner with a cluster of junipers and a couple of big rocks for landscaping. He was pretty sure the place he remembered was just up here.

"We could use some carpenters in the Siksika Valley," she said. "The Amish community is growing every year, with more families moving in and opening businesses."

"Andrew is a partner in the business, too," he reminded her. "It's more likely that you'll be moving to Amity, isn't it? Since he seems to have made up his mind to live an Amish life. Again." Finally.

"What does that mean?"

Surely Andrew had told her. And if he hadn't, it wasn't a big secret. "He's left home twice before to live *Englisch*."

"But last summer—he was in church with both of you. He went to all the doings with the *Youngie*." Her face in the depths of the bonnet turned up toward him, and her grey eyes were puzzled. "That was only six and a half months ago."

So precise. Six and a *half* months.

"That's what I don't understand," he said. "Was that when things began with you? Because I don't remember him courting anyone in particular. And I'm pretty sure I was there."

He had time to see her blush scarlet before she looked away. "I believe you were. But I bet you don't remember seeing me, do you?"

He was saved from having to correct her by their arrival at the bed and breakfast. It was an old-fashioned, bungalow style house with a wraparound porch and an oriel window over the front door. They'd used the original colors from the 1920s, which always pleased him. It was kind of sad to see a gracious old lady of a house painted turquoise with purple trim, or some other modern combination. The hand-carved sign at the gate read, Blackberry Cottage B&B.

The proprietor was a young woman with a toddler on her

hip. "Sure," she said, taking in their Amish clothes. "I'd be glad to have you. We don't get many visitors at this time of year. I'm Rosalie Garcia. Come in and have a look."

The rooms were spacious and comfortable, and no more expensive than any of the motels he'd stayed in from time to time.

"So you and your wife can have the one with the ensuite," their hostess said, "and who will be in the second room? Will they mind using the bath here on the main landing?"

For a moment Noah's mouth forgot how to form words. From his brother's fiancé to his own wife—what was it with Rebecca Miller, anyway?

"We're not married," Rebecca said hastily. "Noah and my father will take the one with twin beds, and I'll have the other, if that's all right. Dad is at the hospital with my mother right now—she's in labor and they want to keep her for observation after the baby is born."

This was the most he'd ever heard her say, which didn't help his ability to form a coherent sentence one bit.

"Your mom is in labor?" Rosalie said. "How old are you?"

"I'm twenty-three, and my youngest brother is twenty-one. So it's been a while. But we can't wait to meet the baby."

"Boy or girl?"

"Girl. We're calling her Deborah."

Their hostess smiled in delight. "That's almost this little one's name. Say hi, Debra." She joggled her, and the toddler hid her face from the strangers. "Come on, let's get you registered and settled in."

For a wonder, Rosalie had a supply of toiletries on hand— toothbrushes, toothpaste, shampoo, even deodorant. And there was a generous plate of cookies on the sideboard, along with a basket of potato chips and a bowl of apples. She understood completely about sudden trips to the hospital and lack of preparation. "About half our guests who aren't on vacation or passing through are people with family in the hospital. I learned after a while to keep a stock on hand—and toiletries don't go bad, do they?"

Noah paid her in cash for the two rooms, and when she lit the fire in the common room, it drew him and Rebecca in like a pair of moths.

"I can't get too comfortable," Rebecca said, holding out her hands to the crackling flames, "or I'll curl up right here on the rug like a cat, and go to sleep."

"Neither of us had a proper sleep last night, it seems," he said. She had long, slender fingers, and the firelight made them blush around the edges. "We drove straight through to save on motel rooms." He told her about arriving at the Gingerich place only to be told about Andrew, and turning right around to head back to Libby.

"So that's how you all appeared so quickly," she said, as though she'd been wondering. "Well, when he wakes up, he'll be glad to see the people he loves."

Would he? When Noah was silent, she glanced at him curiously.

He gazed into the flames so he wouldn't have to meet her eyes. "Andrew has been having a rough time," he said at last. "He left home a couple of years ago, when we were all living in Kentucky. Then he came back, and we thought a new adventure in Colorado would help settle him. Just us three boys, starting a business together." He hesitated, uncertain of how much she knew. "Maybe he's told you he and Dat don't get along so well."

47

"Neh," she said softly. "This is all news to me."

"He probably wanted to put it all behind him," Noah admitted. "Anyway, Mamm and Dat sold up and made plans to move here. Andrew was supposed to come ahead to get the place ready for them. Except ..."

"He didn't," Rebecca said. "I'd have noticed."

"What was he doing all that time? And how did he end up in somebody's car?"

She turned away and collected her coat from the sofa. "I don't know. Come on, we'd better go. Visiting hours will be half over by the time we get back to the hospital, and I want to know if the *Boppli* has arrived yet."

He pushed down a surge of frustration at still having no answers. But she was right. It was time to go back. They had to walk quickly because the temperature was dropping, so it was difficult to exchange confidences. But still ... surely she must understand his confusion about Andrew's whereabouts. If he hadn't been with Rebecca and working on the house, had he gone somewhere else? And how did that car fit into the picture? Who had been driving?

He was beginning to think that the only person with all the answers was Andrew. And only *der Herr* knew when he would wake up to enlighten them all.

THANK goodness their need to return to the hospital distracted Noah, or Rebecca would have broken down right there by the fire, and 'fessed up to her deceit of him and his family.

You have to straighten this out. You can't let it go on. You've turned yourself into a liar because you're a coward, Rebecca Miller.

How had she gotten herself into this? She was trapped in a tangled web, that was sure and certain. She should have corrected that nice nurse's assumption right off the bat, and none of this would have happened. But she hadn't, and soon Dat and Mamm were going to get wind of it, and then she'd be in the soup.

But oh, how happy Andrew's mother had been. She had practically wept with joy at the thought of Andrew settling down and choosing the Amish way for good and ever. Choosing salvation rather than risking hellfire. How on earth was Rebecca going to tell the truth to that poor woman, and watch the joy fade out of her eyes?

But she had to. Before Andrew woke up and made it plain to everyone that he had no idea who she was. She would have to endure the humiliation and shame she'd brought on herself, and suffer her parents' disappointment in her for months. Probably years.

In the waiting room of the maternity ward, she bit back a groan.

She would be ninety years old and still someone would bring up the story of how she'd faked an engagement to a man in a coma who didn't even know her name. She would never, ever be able to live this down.

She buried her face in her hands.

"Rebecca? *Liewi*, it's all right. Your mother is fine. It all went well, and she's comfortable now in the recovery room."

Rebecca raised her head as her father sat down beside her and slipped an arm around her shoulders.

"Little Deborah is well and healthy. You should be able to go in and see her soon."

She hid her face in his shoulder and burst into tears.

"It's all right," he murmured, patting her back. "Mamm is fine. Both of them are."

Oh, Dat, if only you knew what a mess I've made!

But how selfish she was, thinking of her own idiocy and not of Mamm, who had just endured childbirth when she'd thought she was long past it. "I'm so glad," she gulped, choking down her tears.

He peered into her face. "It's been a long day for you, too, hasn't it? What are you still doing here? I thought you went home with Liam hours ago."

She shook her head. "There wasn't room in the truck."

"For two people? It's a pretty big truck."

And then her tired brain remembered that he knew nothing about the Kings' arrival, or of Andrew's condition.

"She gave up her seat so that my parents, my oldest brother, and my two sisters could go back to Mountain Home and get some rest," Noah's voice came from the doorway of the waiting room. He strolled over to them, seated himself in the chair nearest Dat, and held out a hand. "Noah King."

Dat shook his hand, looking a little bemused. "Reuben Miller. Maybe you'd like to explain what's going on."

"I thought you knew," he said. "Aendi Annie said you'd called to say that Rebecca and my brother Andrew had come down here in the ambulance."

Dat's face cleared—and it was obvious that in the excitement of little Deborah's arrival, he'd forgotten all about the other Amish patient in the hospital. "Ah, you're one of those Kings."

Noah chuckled. "Yes, those Kings."

"How is *dei bruder?*" Dat asked.

"As well as can be expected, I guess. Rebecca knows more than I do."

Dat turned to gaze at her curiously. "You do?"

She swallowed. "He had a dislocated shoulder and a fractured tibia. A little hypothermia, too. But they set his bones and now we just have to wait for him to wake from his coma. They had to sedate him because his brain is a bit swollen."

"We?" Dat said, looking more and more mystified at all this knowledge.

Noah's lips curved in a smile. "I hear we're all going to be family soon."

Rebecca made a convulsive movement, as if her hands wanted to press themselves over his mouth without any prompting from her brain. "Noah—"

"How is that?" Dat asked.

Noah nodded at Rebecca, who sat there helplessly as the avalanche of consequences roared down the mountainside of deceit, straight at her.

"Because my brother Andrew is going to marry Rebecca here. They've been engaged, apparently, for months, with none of us the wiser."

CHAPTER 6

*N*aomi Miller cuddled the sweet warmth of her youngest daughter against her chest to give herself a moment to think after her older daughter's revelation a moment ago. Her body might ache tomorrow, but today she could only think how miraculous it was that little Deborah had rooted at her breast, found a good latch, and been able to nurse. Now satisfied, the newborn in her arms was content and sleepy.

Naomi finally raised her eyes to her husband and daughter.

"I don't understand," she said to Rebecca. So quiet. So unobtrusive and self-effacing that her kindnesses to others often went overlooked—or were attributed to someone else. "You're engaged? How? When?"

"I—well, I—" Rebecca's tongue got tangled and Naomi turned her gaze on her husband.

"How is it we didn't know?"

He shrugged helplessly, then held out his arms for the baby. Naomi put her into them and her heart squeezed at the tenderness in those callused rancher's hands as he cradled her head and supported her tiny neck. His face was soft and touched with surprise, as though love had ambushed him, too, the way it had Naomi, an unstoppable wave they welcomed as it washed through them. "My little Easter miracle," he murmured to Deborah, and kissed her forehead.

Then he did his best to come back to the present. "Most of the *Youngie* don't say much. We didn't, *Liewi*, if you remember. Some parents don't find out their children are planning to be married until the week before it's published in church."

"But we aren't some parents," Naomi protested. "Daniel and Lovina told us right away. And Joshua made such a spectacle of himself over Sara it would be hard to miss it. Though I'm glad they're waiting until November. Best to settle into church life first, after running from it half their lives."

Easter Sunday was tomorrow. Joshua, Sara, and the twins had been in baptism classes for sixteen weeks, and on New Birth Sunday two weeks from now, they would be baptized together. Four souls would come to God, fresh and new, their sins washed away in the blood of the Lamb, and carried into the sea of God's forgetfulness.

Naomi gathered her scattered thoughts. "You're to be baptized on New Birth Sunday too, *Liebschdi*, with Malena," she said to Rebecca. "Of course a young person must be baptized before they are married in church, but—but is that why you chose to be baptized now? Because you accepted this young man?" She gazed at her daughter a little helplessly.

It was so difficult not to feel hurt that Rebecca hadn't confided in her. They could have shared so much. She could have been giving help and advice all this time. Treated her like a wife-to-be, not a daughter who would rather be out in the fields with the horses or in the hens' aviary than go to a volleyball game.

Maybe that was why she'd been so reticent this winter. Not wanting to join much of the doings of the *Youngie*. Because other than being with her buddy bunch, there wasn't much point in making herself available for a ride home in someone's buggy after singing. Because she'd already made her choice. Been chosen.

Her Rebecca. Her shy sparrow with the sweet spirit had been chosen by a man they didn't even know.

"Oh, child." She pressed the button that would raise the head of the bed some more, and held out her arms. Rebecca leaned into them, her face hot in the crook of Naomi's shoulder. "I'm so happy for you. When can we meet the young man? When can we hear all about it?"

"You can meet him now, though he won't know it," Rebecca mumbled into her hospital gown before she straightened. "He's on the second floor, sedated in Intensive Care. From the accident."

Good heavens. "Do they expect him to wake up soon?"

Rebecca shrugged. "He's healthy and there were no internal injuries. Just his head, when it struck the ice in the Siksika River, and the bones."

"When he was thrown from the car," Reuben reminded her. "Remember what Adam told us? Rebecca got him to the fire station, and they brought him down here."

It was coming back to her now. "Was that only last night?" she wondered aloud. "It seems like a year ago."

"You've been kind of busy since yesterday," Rebecca said with a smile. "Dat, can I hold her?"

Reuben transferred the baby into Rebecca's arms and she

smiled down at her tiny *schweschder* with such tenderness that Naomi couldn't help but glance at her husband. His eyes twinkled. They were both thinking the same thing. *She is going to make a wonderful mother.*

It was hard to imagine slender Rebecca wrestling an unconscious man up that bank and heaving him into a buggy. Was that what love did? Love and the strength of God, both combining to work a miracle?

"But what was he doing in a car?" Naomi said. "Was it an *Englisch* taxi?"

Rebecca looked a little concerned. "Mamm, your mind is all over the place. And no wonder—you're exhausted."

Not so exhausted she couldn't ask questions.

Rebecca gave Deborah back to her, and the sleeping baby snuggled once more against her chest. Naomi adored that feeling. Such a tiny little person, yet Naomi could make her feel so safe, so comforted. It wouldn't be long before she was awake again, and already Naomi couldn't wait to provide what the baby needed to thrive and grow.

Yet … her eyelids drooped in spite of themselves.

Reuben leaned over and kissed them both, then pressed the button to lower the bed. "Get some rest, *mei Fraa*," he whispered. "I'll go down and see this young man of hers."

"Mm," Naomi said, and tucked the baby against her chest.

They'd be able to go home tomorrow, if her body proved as resilient as Dr. Gupta predicted it would be. Strong and healthy, she was. And sleepy.

So sleepy… She'd close her eyes just for a moment…

REBECCA and her father found Noah sitting next to Andrew's bed. Had anyone told him that a person in an induced coma might be able to hear? He ought to take advantage of these quiet moments to talk to his brother, to lay the groundwork for bringing peace to the family.

But as usual, the uncomfortable feeling that their family business was none of her concern made her silent. All Rebecca could do was give an uncertain smile as they walked in. The room contained the gentle scent of the shaving cream piled in a bowl under the bed. The nurses used it to mask the smell of bodily fluids and people who couldn't yet have baths. Luckily, Andrew wasn't one of those, but still, there was the bowl, discreetly doing its job.

Noah looked up. "No change," he said, as though someone had asked. "I'm wondering if my brother will be the same man after this as he was before."

"That is in the hands of *der Herr*," Dat said.

For a few moments, they watched Andrew's chest rise and fall. Rise and fall. The ventilator was helping him breathe. Reuben examined Andrew's face, as if he might discern the kind of man he was by sight alone. But even Rebecca couldn't do that. She'd examined his face to her heart's content in Colorado and even last night, and she was no closer to knowing his character than what Noah had told her of him this afternoon.

"I understand your family has gone back to Mountain Home," Dat said to Noah at last. "I suppose Rebecca and I had best be thinking the same."

"Dat," Rebecca said, "Noah and I booked rooms for the three of us in a bed and breakfast place this afternoon, since they want to keep Mamm overnight."

"You did?" Her father gazed at her, his eyebrows rising. "What possessed you to do that? What about your baptism class tomorrow?"

"I'm sure Bishop Joe knows our situation," she said. "I'll make up the lesson before New Birth Sunday."

"Getting rooms seemed sensible," Noah said, coming to her rescue. "I saw the place on the way in. You and I are sharing, and Rebecca has her own. I hope that's all right."

"You'll let me pay my share," Dat said in a tone that brooked no argument.

"There's no rush. But if either of us were needed in the night at the hospital, I thought it would be best if we were close at hand."

Rebecca could see in her father's face that he hadn't thought that far ahead just yet. He was probably thinking of the calves, but her brothers were well able to take care of them. "Our job is to be here for Mamm," she said, leaning on his shoulder as they stood side by side. *"Kumm mit.* Visiting hours are over soon, and they're strict about booting people out at exactly five o'clock."

They found some supper in the cafeteria downstairs, and then made their way back to Blackberry Cottage, where a fresh plate of chocolate chip cookies waited and Dat was shown where he and Noah would be sleeping. At seven, Dat gave Rebecca a one-armed hug and then made his way up the staircase, his weathered hand caressing the glossy wood as though it were a horse's hide.

"Don't stay up too late," he warned, then smiled at her before he climbed the rest of the way. Poor Dat. The slow thud of his rancher's boots on the stairs told her more about his weariness than any expression in his face.

She, on the other hand, should have been tired, but wasn't. Maybe this was what people called getting your second wind. She joined Noah in the sitting room, where he put a couple of pieces of wood on the fire, dusted off his hands, and sat on the sofa gazing at the logs as they caught.

"We could watch TV if one of us could figure out how to turn it on," he said, half joking.

"I haven't been in baptism classes for fourteen weeks to pretend I'm still on *Rumspringe*," she told him, sinking into the other corner of the sofa. The fire felt good.

"I was kidding. Just you?"

She shook her head. "My sister and I. And my youngest brother Joshua and his intended, Sara. Bishop Joe says it's the biggest crowd he's had in years."

Noah smiled. "It's a small community?"

"Getting bigger every year, like I told you. But it's hard for the *Youngie* here to really get out and run wild, because there's only one little bar and two restaurants in Mountain Home. You have to drive forty miles every time you want to kick up your heels. That gives you time for second thoughts." She paused. "Though Joshua never seemed to have any difficulty ignoring them. He was friends with the boys on the dude ranch up the road from us. The Rocking Diamond. A truck makes things like a ski trip to Whitefish possible, where without one, you'd have to be satisfied with sleighriding down the hill behind the house, or playing pond hockey."

"Those sound like fun," Noah said. "Is that what you like to do?"

With a smile, she nodded. "I like to skate. The river winds and slows down below our house, so it freezes hard. I can skate for a mile before it gets close to the lake and it's not so safe."

"Andrew is good at hockey," he said, settling back in the sofa's comfortable embrace. "And skiing, and snowshoeing. He's a sportsman. Likes to hunt and fish. Play games in teams. He's the kind that always gets picked to be captain. My oldest brother Simeon ought to be, but Andrew seems to have a knack for it. Sim just gets bossy and people wander away."

"Poor Sim. Does it hurt his feelings?"

"No one knows," Noah said. "Sim doesn't show much. Neither does Andrew, if it comes to that. Not a lot of talkers in our family, except Mamm and the girls."

"Dat isn't either. But he feels things deeply." Then she wondered if that might have offended her companion. "I didn't mean—"

He waved a hand. "I know what you meant. It's funny. Andrew is a people person, but he's not very good at opening up. I'm not really a people person, and yet here I am, talking to you."

And here she was, talking to him, too. "Nobody would ever say I was a people person," she admitted. "People tend to forget I'm there."

"Until now," Noah pointed out. "I know you're here. Andrew knows you're here when you're next to his bed, I'm sure. And my parents do. They're probably thanking *der Herr* on their knees for you right now."

She felt her cheeks heat up in a blush. Maybe he would think it was because of the warmth of the fire.

"Mamm has been so afraid for him over the last couple of years," he said, contemplating the flames. "I'd have letters from her that made me think she was going to get sick over it. You know what really got to me? She left a lamp in the kitchen window for him every time he left, to guide him back. A cousin of hers in Whinburg Township did that for her children, too. And they did come back." He glanced at her. "This last time, we learned he went to Denver, and got work on a construction crew. Then we heard he was working on a ski hill west of there, running the lift. Then he couldn't stand being away from the family and came home. Put on Amish clothes and went to church. So we brothers decided to go to Amity for a fresh start. See if that would help him, like I said before, with no parents looking over his shoulder. And for a while, it worked. He seemed happy." Another look over at her. "That was probably because of you."

"And what happened?" She hardly dared ask.

"Nothing, that we knew of." He pushed himself higher on the cushions, and reached for another cookie. "Mamm and Dat sold up and made plans to move here, and we thought everything was fine. Now I find he's engaged to you and everything really is fine. Better than fine. Until the accident." His gaze turned from the fire to her. "Who do you think was driving that car? Was it really just an *Englisch* taxi, taking him somewhere? But where would he go, without you? And why isn't he being baptized with you? Is he waiting for the autumn Communion for some reason? Or will he take that step in Amity, where the bishop knows him?"

"I—I don't know," she managed. The ease of their conversation drained away like dishwater going down the sink. She needed to confess her sin or run away, both of which would spoil the evening completely.

"Was he meeting you? Was that why you were right there

when the accident happened? Why didn't the driver stay to help?"

At least she could tell the truth about that, unsatisfying as it was.

"I don't know, Noah. I was coming home from helping Sara at her hay farm, and the car spun out, and the next thing I knew, he was flying out the car door, down the slope and onto the ice."

Silence fell, though she could practically hear him going through her words the way she combed burrs out of Marigold's tail, a few strands at a time.

"He must have been going somewhere in a taxi, and just didn't have time to tell you," he said at last. "When he wakes up, we'll get the whole story."

"Ja," she croaked.

Oh, just tell him. It's just the two of you. And he'll never speak to you again and it will be everything you deserve.

Then she had a horrible thought.

If it gets out, will it prevent me from being baptized?

But if she said nothing, and was baptized with such a sin on her conscience, no amount of water on her head in front of the whole congregation would wash that sin away in God's eyes.

She had to tell. If she wanted to join church, she couldn't let this go on. First Noah, now, and then tomorrow, Dat and Mamm.

The fire popped and made her jump, like a rodeo horse at a starting gun. "Noah, I need to tell you something."

He gazed at her curiously.

She took a deep breath to calm her heart. "I'm not engaged to Andrew."

Now his curious gaze deepened into real astonishment and even disbelief. "Not engaged? You mean, the two of you are already married?"

Oh, help us! If she hadn't been sitting down already, her knees might have given out on her. "We're not married, either. We're nothing. We're not a *we* at all."

His mouth moved, as though words were trying to get out, and finally he just stared.

How could she explain?

"It was a mistake. A nurse heard me say something and misunderstood. If I hadn't said it in *Englisch*, none of this would have happened."

"Said what? What did you say?"

She shook her head, helplessly. "I don't even remember. But she started telling people we were engaged, and that's why they let me stay in the ICU with him, because I was immediate family, and then suddenly there you were, his actual family, and she told you all, too, and—and—it's all been this big snowball and I didn't know how to stop it."

He shook his head, as though she'd slapped him and made his ears ring. "You didn't know how to stop it. It didn't occur to you to open your mouth and say, wait, it's not true, it's all a mistake?"

"It did, lots of times, but I never got the chance."

"I can't believe this. How are you going to tell my mother? I just told you she thinks you walk on water because with you, Andrew will settle down and join church. And now to find out it's all a lie? It will break her heart."

Rebecca moaned and covered her face. "I know. I'm so sorry. I—"

He leaped to his feet. "I guess you *are* sorry. *Sorry* doesn't even begin to cover it. I can't believe you could do such a thing to us."

"I didn't do anything!" she cried, tears overflowing and trickling down her cheeks. "Not on purpose."

"That's right," he said, as though remembering something important. "Doing nothing can be as great a sin as doing something, can't it?"

She could take no more, not in that rough tone full of pain, especially when he was right and she had brought this down on herself by her own foolishness. She fled the warmth of the fire, ran up the stairs, and locked herself in her pretty paid-for room. Brushed her teeth. Took down her hair. Cried in the shower. Washed her underthings and hung them over the radiator to dry.

Knelt by the bed and tried to pray. Failed.

Finally she just climbed into bed and lay there, staring at the shapes the city lights made on the ceiling, until she heard Noah's quiet steps go past her door.

Even the sound felt like a reproach.

CHAPTER 7

*R*osalie Garcia dished up the kind of breakfast you couldn't help but remember and tell your friends about—cheesy muffins with flecks of green chile, *huevos rancheros*, fruit salad, and a bottomless pot of excellent coffee with fresh cream. But Noah was hardly in a state of mind to appreciate the food in the way it deserved. While he'd only managed to get a couple of hours of sleep and could barely bring himself to say *guder mariye* to her, Rebecca ate quickly, mechanically, in between chipping out sentences to her father that were clearly painful, over the cheery breakfast dishes.

When she confessed, she didn't do it by halves.

When she was finished, Reuben Miller helped himself to some more coffee and gazed at his daughter. Noah fully expected the same sad look he'd so often seen on his own father's face after hearing about one of his or his brothers' thoughtless escapades. But he couldn't read this man's expression.

Then again, Reuben probably hadn't run up against anything like this before.

How could Rebecca have misled them like this? How could she have kept quiet and let the lie grow and grow, until it had wrapped his mother's heart in its deceptive sweetness, distracted his sisters with the possibility of happy endings, and even made Simeon believe—however briefly—that love could conquer all?

Noah could just shake her for what this news was going to do to his family.

He was shaking inside from what it had done to him. Was this the real Rebecca? Not the shy, sweet-natured person she had shown herself to be on the outside, but a schemer who had taken advantage of his brother's situation to insinuate herself into his family? He couldn't for the life of him figure out why she might do that, when she had a loving family of her own. But maybe she was the kind of woman who enjoyed being the center of attention. Who craved it. Who would do anything, even the outrageous, to get it.

She and Andrew were two peas in a pod, if that were the case. Andrew never saw the grief in his parents' hearts when he left home. He only saw the joy when he returned. Joy that soothed the jagged edges of a heart that couldn't be satisfied with the Amish life. That wanted more and then even more.

Was Rebecca like that, too? This slender young woman whose head was bowed over her empty plate while, even as he watched, a tear dripped off the tip of her nose?

He rolled his eyes at himself as he handed her the large paper napkin from the unused fourth place setting.

She blew her nose and mopped her face without looking at him. Well, he didn't want her to look at him. He'd likely be drawn in by those eyes, too, and then he really would be in a pickle.

Reuben Miller set down his coffee. "I can see there's no need for me to say anything," he mused aloud, watching his daughter with eyes filled with compassion. "You've done a fair enough job of punishing yourself. And I don't doubt you've thought through what you might do next."

The white *Kapp* on the bowed head bobbed up and down.

"I can't say your mother will be sorry." He glanced at Noah. "No offense to *dei Bruder*, son."

Noah could only shake his head. After the offense Rebecca had dealt the family, this was nothing.

"It will clear up the little mystery about why you wouldn't have told us." He gazed at her. "I have to admit I couldn't believe you could keep such a secret for so long without its getting out somehow. Either from yourself, or through the Amish grapevine."

"I couldn't even keep it for twenty-four hours," she said hoarsely. "My conscience wouldn't let me."

"It's a pity your conscience didn't act sooner," came out of Noah's mouth before he could stop it. He had a mad urge to apologize for his rudeness, but bit back the words.

"It is a pity," Reuben agreed mildly, to Noah's surprise. "At least before your family heard. But Rebecca will confess it to them when we get home."

"But Dat—the baptism—?" She choked and couldn't go on.

"You made a mistake, and you have done and will do your best to mend it," Reuben told her gently. "If *der Herr* can forgive, and the Kings can forgive, then the bishop has no cause to exclude you."

"And if the Kings can't forgive?" Rebecca asked miserably. "If I've hurt them more than they can bear?"

Noah was sitting right there, representing the family. She might have asked him.

"Then that would be on their conscience, *Dochder*," Reuben said. "Your duty before *Gott in Himmel* is to ask their forgiveness. Their duty is to give it from an honest and compassionate heart."

Noah's own heart gave a kind of clutch in his chest. Was Reuben speaking directly to him? Did the weatherbeaten rancher know that he was holding this shocked resentment in his heart on his family's behalf, holding it close as though it were a kitten whose claws could scratch without warning?

Was his unforgiveness as silent a sin as her doing nothing had been?

Noah buried his nose in his coffee mug so he wouldn't have to answer his own conscience.

"In the meanwhile, we'll go along to the hospital," Reuben went on. "See when they're going to discharge your mother and sister so we can go home."

"I'll phone Liam once we know." She sounded hesitant, as though she could hardly believe they could speak of ordinary things once again.

"*Neh*, the boy did enough for us yesterday," Reuben said. "There's a man here in town who doesn't mind giving Amish folks a ride. I'll see if he's available."

They collected their few belongings, thanked Rosalie Garcia for her good care of them, and walked over to the hospital. There, Noah left Rebecca to explain herself to her mother and the baby, and took himself off to the ICU and his brother.

Nothing had changed since last night, except maybe the bowl of shaving cream, which looked as though it were slowly deflating. The monitors still beeped, the numbers on the screen still showed heart rate and oxygen levels, and Andrew still lay, his lashes thick crescents that used to make *die Maedscher* swoon. Somehow they never seemed to see the eyes that looked away, over the fence to a car, possessions, clothes—a life that was not Amish.

He sank into the chair next to the bed.

"Guder mariye, Andrew," he said. His brother's chest rose and fell in a regular, peaceful rhythm. "Once again you're in the middle of a fine to-do. That girl we thought you were engaged to? Rebecca Miller? She is quite the piece of work. Mamm and Dat were so happy. So were Clara and Patricia. Even Sim cracked a smile at the news. We all thought you were going to get married and join church. And now it turns out—"

A nurse came in and smiled at him. "You're his brother, aren't you?"

He nodded. "Noah King."

"Nice to meet you, Noah. I'm Sasha. I was here when your brother and his fiancée came in Friday night."

Was this the nurse who had started the whole misunderstanding?

He cleared his throat. "Turns out she's not actually his—"

The phone rang outside at the nurse's station, and she tapped the door frame. "Sorry. I'm alone until Judy comes back from the restroom."

She went to answer the phone and he subsided into the chair.

Was it this easy? Interruptions, distractions, a silent second, and a lie got away on you and had time and space to grow. He'd had every intention of clearing up the mess with

68

one firm sentence, and now look. The nurse had gone back to work and the mess had not changed one bit.

He hoped Rebecca was having better luck upstairs in the maternity ward.

He gazed at his brother. His heart squeezed with love—for the boys they had been. Stairsteps at eight, six, and four. The boys sandwiched between two sets of girls. Sim and Andrew had let Noah tag along to the creek with them, and taught him to swim and to fish long before Dat had got around to thinking of it. They had walked him to school on his first day, so happy to be a scholar at last, like them. And they hadn't even abandoned Noah in the schoolyard to go play baseball with their friends, but had stuck by him until he'd been introduced to the teacher and assigned to a desk. Climbing trees, turning over the garden, learning to drive the horses ... Andrew had been the best brother a boy could ask for.

And now? Noah couldn't imagine what the future held.

Not a wedding, for sure and certain.

His gaze returned to his brother's face. Andrew's eyelids twitched, as though he were trying to blink with his eyes closed. The fingers lying on the soft blue coverlet moved.

Noah drew a breath, glancing out at the nurse's station. *Ja*, there were two of them there now.

When he looked back, Andrew's eyes were open. Staring up at the ceiling. Trying to figure out where he was?

Noah leaped out of the chair and Andrew's gaze swung to him. With the respirator in, he couldn't speak, but his eyebrows rose in surprise.

"Nurse!" Noah croaked. He couldn't remember her name. Three big steps took him to the door. "Nurse, he's awake! My brother is awake!"

CHAPTER 8

*R*ebecca left her parents with the happy task of filling out Deborah's birth certificate—or rather, Mamm fed the baby while Dat and the administrator filled it out. The last fifteen minutes of Rebecca's second confession of the day had not been easy, but Mamm had seemed relieved to know that Rebecca wasn't keeping secrets from her, large or small.

Her relationship with her parents had always been close. Mamm and Dat always said that they had no favorites among their children, but Rebecca knew Dat always had a little extra time for her, and Joshua had broken Mamm's heart more than once, if the soft weeping behind her parents' bedroom door in the last year or two was any indication. But all that was behind Joshua and Sara now. With Daniel's wedding to Lovina Lapp coming up at the end of the month, after the baptism, it added even more to her parents' happiness.

And now little Deborah was added to their family, and would be a playmate for Joshua's Nathan when they got a little older.

All the same, Rebecca was relieved to leave her parents alone with the baby. She'd just run down to the ICU to see if there was any change in Andrew's condition. It was too much to expect to find him without a visitor, but even after that horrible scene last night, surely Noah wouldn't begrudge her looking in to see how his brother was?

She slipped into the glassed-in room to find Noah and the nurses bending over Andrew's bed. When one of the nurses straightened to check the monitor, Rebecca stopped in her tracks.

Andrew was awake.

He hadn't seen her yet. If she took just two steps, she'd be back outside the door and no one would know she'd even been there.

One step. Two—

"Excuse me, miss." A doctor in a white coat steadied her as he brushed past on his way to Andrew's bed. "I hear he's over-breathing the vent. That's a great sign."

Andrew's gaze slid from Rebecca to the doctor, then back to Rebecca.

Oh, no. Now was a fine time for him to notice her at last!

Rebecca stepped out of the door, but stood just outside so she could hear and see a little. Overbreathing the vent—that was *gut*? Did it mean he could breathe outside its steady rhythm? Breathe by himself already?

"Nice to have you back with us," the doctor said to Andrew, glancing among the monitors that couldn't help but tell the truth. "We're going to run some tests now that you're awake, and if everything checks out, we'll get that ventilator pulled. Seems you might not need it anymore."

After a moment, Noah said, "He's fallen asleep again. He hasn't gone into a coma, has he?"

"I don't think so. We've lightened up on the sedation, that's all," the doctor said. "We're going to restrain him, though, in case he wakes again and wants to get up, or pull out the vent. His body isn't going to do what he wants, and we don't want him to hurt himself. Are you a family member?"

"Yes, his brother," Noah said.

"And his fiancée is waiting outside," the nurse added.

Rebecca closed her eyes briefly. Talk about rubbing salt in Noah's wounds. Did they have to keep bringing it up?

"Mr King, maybe I could speak to you and the young lady, then."

Before Rebecca could make herself disappear, they came out and walked a little way down the corridor. Nurses brushed past, carts rattled by loaded with medications, and visitors spoke softly with their loved ones in the other rooms. But Rebecca could only see Noah's face, and the tightness of his lips.

The accusation in his eyes.

"I'm not his fiancée," Rebecca blurted as she joined them. "It's just a mistake."

The doctor frowned. "All right, if you say so. I want to tell you a little about what to expect here."

Rebecca, thankful to be silent, waited.

"We believe that a patient in a coma, induced or not, can hear what's said to him. I've seen you around the ICU over the last day or two, Miss…?"

"Rebecca," she whispered.

"Rebecca. The nurses all think you're engaged to this man, and whether or not he thinks that, we believe he may have heard conversations to that effect. Did you speak to him as though you were in a relationship of some kind?"

Could she simply drop through the floor now? "Yes," she said. Her cheeks burned, as though Noah's gaze were scalding them.

Noah made a muffled sound and turned away.

"If he comes to full consciousness, he may believe that you are engaged. He may not. He may remember what happened to cause his injuries, or he may not. The point is, whatever he believes is the truth, just for now, I don't think you should argue with him. Or agitate him. Memory will come back in time, but the initial disorientation will be painful enough for him without contradictions for which he has no context. Do you understand what I'm saying?"

Noah cleared his throat. "Whatever he says when he can finally speak, we're to act as if it's normal. Play along, even."

"Stick as close to reality as you can without making him anxious. He was out for a very short time, as these things go, but with even a little swelling of the brain, we have to be cautious. By no means are we going to let him out of here until we know what's what. I just wanted to prepare you."

"Thank you," Rebecca found the wit to say.

"If the tests check out and he can breathe and eat on his own, then we'll move him over to the ward. I wish we had a neuro step-down unit, but we'll make do. He may have hallucinations from the meds, so be prepared for those. Again, don't argue, but encourage him by talking instead about things that are real in his surroundings."

Don't argue. Play along. That was *Englisch* for *lie*, wasn't it? Rebecca was tempted to bang the back of her head against the wall that was holding her up. If she'd just kept her mouth shut and *not* confessed to her foolishness to Noah and her parents, she might still be playing along, but nobody else would. Everyone would believe she and Andrew were engaged, and behave toward them as though it were normal.

But no. She couldn't have gone another hour deceiving her parents like that.

And Noah?

The doctor went back into Andrew's room and finally, Noah's gaze met hers.

"So," he said at last. "Don't argue. Play along."

"I guess so."

"You know what this means, don't you?"

Could he be any more vague? She shook her head.

"It means that if what the doctor says might be true, *I'm* going to be telling your lie now. To that nurse. To Andrew. And what happens when my family comes? Am I going to tell it to them, too?"

"You'll tell them the truth," Rebecca whispered.

"How? That's another four people who have to remember not to argue. To play along. How many have to join in, telling your lie, before my brother is able to distinguish what's real and what's not?"

Her parents. His parents. His sisters and brother. The nurse.

She covered her face with her hands and rubbed her burning eyes.

Oh, what a tangled web we weave when first we practice to deceive. But she hadn't meant to deceive! She'd just never had a chance to tell the truth.

"For him, being engaged to you is going to be just one more hallucination." And with a glare that felt almost like hurt, not recrimination, Noah turned his back on her and went into his brother's room.

A person who can't forget is worse than one who can't remember. Her grandmother used to say that. If Andrew was the one who couldn't remember, was Noah going to be the one who would never forget that she had roped him into a lie?

There didn't seem to be anything more to do but to go back up to Mamm's room and see if she could do something for her.

"They're going to keep me another day," Mamm told her, the bed cranked up so that she could feed Deborah comfortably. "Your father has walked up to the bed and breakfast to arrange another night."

"For all three of us?" Rebecca said before she could stop herself. "Oh, Mamm, I've made such a mess of things."

Her mother patted the side of the bed, and Rebecca sank onto it.

"Andrew is beginning to wake up."

Mamm's brows rose. "That's *gut*, ain't so? It would be terrible for him to be in that state for weeks or even months, poor boy."

"Ja, ischt gut. But the doctor just told us that whatever he believes when he wakes up completely, we're not to argue with him or contradict him."

Mamm gazed at her, waiting. Comfortable sucking noises came from her little sister, under the peach-colored blanket over Mamm's shoulder.

"He also said that it's their belief that Andrew can hear while he's unconscious. So he would have heard people talking about us being engaged." Her face flamed. "And the things I said to him when I was in there alone."

"Liebschdi, do you care for this young man?"

She couldn't meet her mother's gaze. "I've been dreaming about him since last summer, when I was with Amanda and her husband. But ... we've never spoken. I don't think he even knows my name. He looked right at me just now and there was nothing—I could have been a nurse standing beside the doctor for all he knew."

At last she mustered the courage to look up.

Her mother's eyes were filled with compassion and a kind of helpless amazement. "What did you say the other night to bring all this on yourself, *Dochder?*"

"I don't even remember," Rebecca wailed. "But just now, the nurse told the doctor *again* that I was his fiancée and you should have seen Noah's face. This isn't going to end. He'll never forgive me for getting his *mamm*'s hopes up, and I'm never going to hear the end of it from Adam and Zach. And Malena—" She groaned. "Malena is going to make such hay with this."

"You leave your brothers and sister to me," Mamm said firmly. "I'm more concerned about the King family."

Miserably, Rebecca nodded. "The worst of it is, if Andrew thinks we're engaged when he's back with us again, the doctor said we're not to contradict him until his brain heals more. And now Noah is angry with me because he can't correct the mistake with his family. There will be so many people playing along ... acting a lie. Especially him."

"What is he like, this Noah?"

Rebecca had to think about that for a minute. "I met him in Colorado, and I think he might have recognized me when he arrived with his family yesterday. We talked a little last night. And that's when I ... told him. About the engagement mistake. He didn't take it well."

"You asked his forgiveness?"

"*Ja.* Dat says my part is to ask. His part is to forgive. But I don't think Noah is there yet."

Mamm shook her head. "Such a fuss over a simple misunderstanding."

"It's not that simple, Mamm." She didn't want her mother thinking badly of Noah or his family. They had been so kind. "Apparently Andrew has left home at least twice before to live *Englisch.* They're so happy thinking we're engaged because to them, it means he's going to settle down and join church."

"Oh." Understanding colored the single word. "That's a heavy burden for my girl to bear—being the means of a man's salvation. That ought to be between a man and *der Herr*, ain't so?"

"Noah says it will break his mother's heart when she finds out it isn't true—and worse, that her youngest son has been lying to her."

"That's the heart of the matter," her mother said softly. She cuddled Deborah, who seemed to have fallen asleep in midsuck. "But she must know the truth, and soon. As soon as the doctor says it is healthy for Andrew," she amended. "We must hope it doesn't get out in the district and become an even larger problem."

"What are the odds it hasn't happened already?" Rebecca gazed at her mother helplessly. "Today is Easter Sunday, and the whole King family will have gone to church with Annie Gingerich."

Mamm's eyes widened, and she pressed her free hand to her lips. *"Ach, neh."*

Oh, no was right.

❧

WHEN VISITING HOURS WERE OVER, they had another uninspired supper in the hospital cafeteria, and Noah walked back to the bed and breakfast with Rebecca and her father. Andrew had opened his eyes a few times, but overbreathing or not, the doctor wasn't satisfied yet that he was actually conscious.

"I'm certain he knew who I was," Noah said to Rebecca, laying a couple of logs on the fire. Rosalie had clearly lit it again when she knew they were coming back. "He looked right at me and even looked a bit surprised." He glanced up to where Rebecca was hovering in the doorway. "I'm not going to bite your head off. You can come in. Shame to waste this wood."

Reuben Miller had already gone upstairs, his steps lighter than last night now that he knew Rebecca's mother would be released tomorrow and they could go home.

Rebecca sidled in, but unlike last night, it seemed she didn't want to share the sofa. Instead, she settled into an armchair set at an angle to it. Separate.

"Are you still angry with me?" she asked. It was clear the words cost her.

With a sigh, he had to admit he wasn't. Not really. "I suppose I'm angry at the situation. How crazy it's getting, with this *don't argue* business."

"It might not be true. The doctors don't know, do they? Andrew might not have heard anything anyone said."

"We can always hope. Then all we have to do is tell my family."

"You don't have to," she said. "If it's anyone's job, it's mine."

He had a sudden vision of slender Rebecca trying to make way against the gale of his family's emotion on the subject, bent forward as though she were in a high wind. He shook his head. "We'll do it together. I haven't said anything to them, either, and I've had a whole day to find a phone and call Annie. I'm just as guilty as you are."

"Are they coming down to see him tomorrow?"

He nodded. "Your father made some calls while you were with your mother. The *Englisch* taxi is going to bring my family down, and then take the three of you back with them. It's a big van, apparently. Seats ten."

She looked a little apprehensive. Locked in a van with the whole King family for forty miles. Whether the the truth was out yet or not, it was going to be difficult.

"I don't want to think about this any more," he said, rubbing his forehead. "Let's talk about something else."

"We could play Chinese checkers." She indicated a shelf holding a dozen board games to one side of the fireplace.

"I don't know how."

Her eyes widened. "You've never played Chinese checkers? Well, let me show you. It's fun, I promise."

The last thing he wanted to do was something as trivial as a silly board game when his brother was lying broken and not in his right mind, and his parents had no decent place to live. He should be in Mountain Home, helping to make their situation better. But Rebecca's eyes had lit up for the first time since he'd met her, and he didn't have the heart to quench the first sign of lifting spirits when it was clear she was doing her best to rally.

She laid out the board on the middle sofa cushion, and they resumed their old places on each end. She was right. The game was a lot like checkers, only on a six-sided star. Each player's triangular point of the star had to be filled with marbles by the opposite player.

Two minutes in, he realized he had better get his head together, or she was going to beat him across the board. And look at that four-step jump she'd just made—she had a marble on his side already.

"Oh, no, you don't," he muttered, and began mapping routes in his mind.

With a chuckle, she used his clever plan to jump two more of her marbles into his triangle. And after that, he was barely able to keep up. Of course she won.

"Another game," he said, putting his marbles back into their wells.

She won the second game, too, but he was only two marbles behind her, and that was because he'd missed spotting a hop path and had to move his marbles one step at a time, limping into their places moments too late.

"Third time's the charm?" she asked, her eyes sparkling in the light of the electric lamps.

The sight stopped his breath for a second. Those eyes, grey and starred with lashes gone red-gold in the firelight. Eyebrows like a pair of birds' wings. A smile, bright with mischief, bringing out a single dimple deep under the apple of her left cheek.

The guilty waif who could make herself disappear had

disappeared with a vengeance, and in her place was a young woman any man with eyes in his head would notice.

She blinked, and the light faded from her face. "Noah? Don't you want to play anymore?"

A thought broadsided him like a runaway hay wagon. She had said herself that she was not engaged to his brother. But what would happen when Andrew recovered, and was himself again? He was the kind of man who attracted young women like bees to honeysuckle. He might take one look at Rebecca and decide she was the girl he wanted to court, after all. He might join church, and ask her to marry him. A lie might become the truth.

She was not his brother's fiancée. At the moment it was all still fiction. But she cared about him, anybody could see that, after what she'd done. She'd saved his life. And here was Noah, trapped on the other side of his family's belief that she and Andrew were a couple. Unless Andrew spurned the Amish life one last time and left their family for good, Noah might not ever get the chance to win her heart.

Wait—what? What was he thinking? He didn't even like her. Not in that way, at least.

Abruptly, he got up. Two of his marbles rolled off the board and down between the sofa cushions.

"*Guder nacht,*" he said, and left her there, gazing after him with eyes full of hurt.

CHAPTER 9

*R*ebecca could hear the Kings arrive in the ICU waiting room on Monday the way you could hear the Canada geese arriving on the ranch after spring breakup. The birds would sail in to land on the Siksika River below the house, squawking and honking and splashing in the water. There might not be any water in the ICU waiting room, but there was plenty of noise.

A few minutes later, she realized there was a different nurse on duty than there had been the other day, because she appeared in the doorway of Andrew's room with only his parents in tow. "Two family members at a time," the nurse said to Rebecca and Noah. "You two can wait outside with the others, please."

Noah hugged his mother, and then to Rebecca's mortification, Kate King took her in her arms as though she had been another daughter. "You're still here, *Liewi*," she murmured in Rebecca's ear. "I was hoping you would be. Watching over him. Letting him know he's loved."

"Noah's been here, too," she managed. That much was the

truth. Then the impatience in the nurse's face made Rebecca scuttle out the door.

In the waiting room, she was engulfed in hugs by Noah's sisters, with Simeon looking on with a worried smile. Noah was right behind her, and thank goodness for that, because he became the focus of the conversation, answering a barrage of questions and leaving Rebecca to fade to the rear of the group.

"I'm going upstairs to see my mother," she said to no one in particular. No one in particular heard her except maybe Noah, but he wasn't saying much to her today anyway.

He probably hadn't liked being beaten at Chinese checkers last night. But she hadn't thought he was the kind to be a poor loser. They were taught as children that the point of a game wasn't to win, but to let everyone participate and have fun. Maybe he simply didn't like a woman being so forward. Did girls in Kentucky and Colorado pretend to let the boys win?

Not that it mattered. She wasn't interested in Noah King, and it was sure and certain the feeling was mutual. If it hadn't been for his resentment at having to *play along* with her lie, he probably wouldn't have noticed her much at all.

He had, however, managed to squeeze out the information at breakfast this morning that he'd decided not to tell his family right away that the engagement wasn't real. If they really did have to keep Andrew calm by not contradicting whatever he believed when he woke up, Noah thought it would be too difficult if all his family members had to remember they were playing a part.

"But what if he *doesn't* think he's engaged, and wakes up to a whole family who think he is?" Dat had wanted to know. He was enjoying his quiche Lorraine, with slices of honeydew melon and blueberry muffins, and more of Rosalie's wonderful coffee.

"I'll tell them then it was all a misunderstanding," Noah had said, and that was that for the rest of the meal.

Rebecca found Dat in the chair next to Mamm's bed, little Deborah sleeping in his arms.

Mamm was up and had her dress on, but was struggling with the snaps.

"Home," Mamm said, as though it were the next best thing to heaven. She offered her front side to Rebecca, who did up the snaps for her. "I can't wait to sleep in my own bed, and for the *Boppli* to meet her brothers and sister."

Rebecca settled Mamm's green cape over the shoulders of her plain maternity dress, and pinned her apron into place at the small of her back. "I'm down to one pin keeping my covering on. Can I borrow some of yours?"

"Of course." Mamm twinkled at her. "You know I always have a few extra in my purse for you *Maedscher*."

"How is Andrew this morning?" Dat asked, handing it to her.

"The Kings arrived, and they're letting them in two at a time. They didn't need me taking up space, so I came up here. When are they releasing you, Mamm?"

"My report card has good marks," she said, fishing two straight pins out of the change pocket of her handbag and handing them to her. "They say I can go anytime after noon. Which can't come soon enough."

Rebecca pinned her *Kapp* in place and loosened its strings so that a bow connected them at the bottom, lying on her chest. None of the *Youngie* wore them tied under the chin like an elderly woman, but it would have come off altogether this morning with only one pin anchoring it in place.

"I've told your mother that we can go back with—" Dat cut himself off at the sight of Patricia King in the doorway.

Her gaze arrowed straight to Rebecca. "Thank goodness I found you." She nodded to Rebecca's parents, then went on breathlessly, "Such a fuss! The nurse undid my brother's restraints to do something or other, and that rascal—what do you think he did?"

Rebecca shook her head, hardly daring to imagine.

"Mamm saw his hands moving upward on his chest under the covers, but she didn't think anything of it. Next thing you know, he's not pulling the vent out of his mouth, he's pulling the hose out of the machine!"

"Oh, no!" Mamm and Dat exchanged a glance, brows raised. She knew exactly what they were thinking. But she couldn't blame him. Even a person be obedient to authority and compliant with a doctor's orders would have a hard time with a big plastic tube down their throat.

"So there's Mamm, trying to keep Andrew from falling out of bed while Dat is trying to reconnect the hose, and the alarms are going off, and oh my goodness, that cranky nurse is so mad at us."

"She'd probably be mad if they were just sitting there praying for him," Rebecca said. "Did she kick everyone out?"

"She did, but some good came of it, at least. The doctor told Dat that because Andrew's vital signs were all good, and he was fighting so hard, that if everything continued to improve, they'd take the tube out today. They may even be doing it now."

"That is *gut* news," Rebecca said. But once the tube was out, would he be able to speak? What would he say? What kind of turn was her life about to take?

It didn't take long for the *gut Gott* to answer her questions. When she and Patricia arrived at Andrew's room, it was empty and the cranky nurse was stripping the bed. She informed them that Andrew had been moved up onto the ward on the floor above. By the time they found his new room, so had the entire King family.

To Rebecca's astonishment, Andrew was sitting up in bed, a heart monitor still hooked up to him. He was sucking on a Popsicle, looking as though all he'd been through in the last three days was a blood draw.

"The Popsicle is for his sore throat," Clara King whispered as they joined the group. "From the vent."

Rebecca again faded backward so that both his sisters stood between her and Andrew. Their mother sat next to the bed, one hand in his, gazing at him as though he might disappear if she took her eyes off him.

"Does he know us?" Patricia asked her father in a low voice.

Andrew swallowed a bite of Popsicle. "Yes, Patricia, I know you."

She gasped and clasped her hands over her chest. "I'm so glad! We didn't know what to expect. We've been so frightened and worried."

Rebecca had just learned something. There had been no damage to Andrew's hearing. Which might mean ...

"The doctor says he's doing well," Kate King said, "but all the same, they can't move him out of here until he's had a brain scan. They're setting that up now."

"But if he can talk and recognize people, that's a *gut* sign, isn't it?" Patricia persisted.

"It is," Simeon said. "But there's a lot they don't know about the brain. And he's been saying some … interesting things."

Andrew finished the Popsicle and handed his mother the stick, stained pink from the flavoring. "There's a lot I don't know about how I got here." His voice sounded a little hoarse. Should he even be talking?

As one, the Kings swung to look at Rebecca. Patricia and Clara moved aside and suddenly there she was, in the one place she'd longed to be for so many months.

The center of Andrew King's attention.

With a frantic glance at the door, for a single second she considered bolting. But then Noah walked over to lean on the doorframe, so casually it had to be on purpose.

Andrew gazed at her, his focus sharpening as her eyes met his. "I know you."

Yes, she thought she said, but no sound came out. She tried again. "*Ja.* Hullo, Andrew."

"You were in my room before. What happened to the kitten?"

Kitten? In the ICU?

And then she remembered. *Don't contradict him.* "Wh- which one?"

"The black one. It was riding around on your shoulder. I saw you out in the hall when the doctor was walking the bears."

Bears?

If these were the hallucinations the doctor meant, she wasn't certain she was capable of playing along.

"She's been sitting by your bed for three days, *mei Sohn*," Kate said soothingly. Clearly she remembered the doctor's instructions: *Don't argue. Bring him around to reality if you can.* "She's been with you since your accident."

"Accident?" He gazed from his mother to Rebecca. "Three days? Was I racing the buggy again?"

"*Neh*, you were thrown from a car," Rebecca said.

He looked astonished. "What happened to Grossdaadi? He was racing the other buggy. Did the car win?"

Rebecca was becoming really concerned about the poor patient's mind.

"Yes, the car won," she said, doing her best to keep her voice level. Practical, but comforting. "Grossdaadi helped me put you in the buggy and take you to the fire station. They brought you down here in the ambulance. Do you know where you are?"

"Simeon says I'm in the hospital in Libby."

Well, that was something.

"What's the last thing you remember?" Arlon King asked.

But Andrew's forehead wrinkled and he didn't reply. Maybe that was a bad question right now. His brain couldn't handle it. His gaze hadn't left her, though. "I do know you."

She nodded. She could practically feel his sisters behind her, bursting to remind him who she was. *Don't say it. Don't.*

"I remember your voice. You said, *Ich liebe dich*. But I bet you weren't talking to the kitten." He gave her an intimate kind of smile, as if they shared a secret.

How could she ever have said such a reckless thing? A wave of embarrassment washed up her chest, her neck, her face, burning its way to the very tips of her ears. "I *was* talking to the kitten," she croaked.

He shook his head. "No, the kitten wasn't there. You were talking to me, just like we are now. You were telling me what the mountains were like. How they were different from Colorado. How we were going to build a house on the river, where we could see them every day." He smiled at her again and this time her knees went weak. Her own foolish words coming out of that beautiful mouth made her want to cry.

At the same time, if she could have moved, she would have fled out into the April afternoon and not stopped running until she reached Blackberry Cottage.

"We've made plans, haven't we?" he said in tones of wonder. "What's your name?"

No, she'd stop running when she got to Mountain Home.

"This is Rebecca, *mei Sohn*," Kate said. "Rebecca Miller. Your intended bride."

"We're getting married?" An expression something like joy was dawning on Andrew's face.

Some part of her was aware that Noah had turned. As if he planned to walk out the door.

Her tongue was frozen to the roof of her mouth with shame and indecision. She needed to stop Noah. To explain she'd never expected Andrew to hear all that, never mind remember it. To beg Noah not to hate her, and remind him they were doing what the doctor said.

But all she could do was smile weakly while Andrew's family surged in to chatter and laugh and congratulate him on remembering.

And when she looked toward the door again, Noah was gone.

CHAPTER 10

I will lift up mine eyes to the hills, from whence cometh my help.

The Psalmist knew what he was talking about, Noah thought, as the *Englisch* taxi van sped northward toward Mountain Home. The Rockies rose into the sky in all their majesty, the snow on their peaks gleaming in the afternoon sun. Below them, the foothills rose and fell, dark with pines and as-yet-leafless aspens, while the river they were following glimmered between the trees.

The sight lifted his spirits as nothing else this week could have done. Only God's handiwork could produce this kind of deep-seated joy.

Rosalie Garcia had been delighted to book his parents a room at Blackberry Cottage for as long as they might need it. "I've got a party of fly fishermen coming the third Saturday in May, when the rivers open, but I'm happy to have drop-ins until then," she'd said cheerfully. So he and Sim and his sisters were heading to their new home to get started at last on the renovations, while Mamm and Dat stayed close to Andrew.

The doctor would need to run a number of scans and tests, now that he was awake, which would likely take the rest of the week.

No one seemed to think it odd that Rebecca and her parents were going home with them, and Rebecca was not keeping vigil by Andrew's bed the way she had done.

But that might change. The doctor had said there was a private neurological rehabilitation clinic not far from Mountain Home, and he would see what he could do to have Andrew transferred there for the longer-term part of his recovery. The question nagged at Noah—would she visit him regularly if he were closer? Would this false engagement become a real one if they spent that much time together?

He gazed at the back of her *Kapp* from his seat in the rear of the van, and let his sisters' excited chatter wash over him. They wanted to know all about the *Youngie* in the district. Sim inquired about what Rebecca had meant when she'd told Andrew about building a house with a view of the mountains. What were land prices like? Which drew Reuben and Naomi Miller into the conversation. Baby Deborah was silent on the subject, tucked into her car seat between her parents, fast asleep.

The faint hope that his family might not have said anything to the district had died almost immediately after they'd climbed into the van. When Naomi had asked after the news from church yesterday, Clara and Patricia had regaled her with how surprised people had been that Rebecca was engaged to someone from Colorado. Noah had seen the Millers' discomfort at not being able to correct the family's misunderstanding.

The doctor may have advised them not to argue with

Andrew about the fantasy engagement, but it irked him beyond bearing to have to deceive his family. In fact, it was unbearable. He'd put a stop to it right now, come what may.

"Simeon," he said, leaning over the seat, "Clara—Pat—listen up. Rebecca has something to tell you."

"I do?" she said, turning in alarm.

"*Ja,*" he told her. "I can't stand it. I won't. This morning's plan was a bad one, and I'm sorry I ever opened my mouth about it. We have to fix this now, while at least part of the family is together in one place."

"I agree," Reuben said.

"That horse got out of the barn a day or two ago," Naomi said, nodding, "but I think it's the right thing, too."

From two seats back, he could see the color creeping up Rebecca's neck, and when she turned in her seat to face his sisters, her cheeks were scarlet.

"The truth is, I'm not engaged to your brother," she said clearly. "It was all a mistake—a misunderstanding by the nurse. When she told you all that first morning that I was his fiancée, I was interrupted—was too embarrassed to correct her—and the damage was done."

Silence. Only the sound of the van's engine could be heard, and the faint sound of the stock report the driver was listening to up front.

Simeon turned to look at Noah. "I don't understand."

His sisters had been stricken silent, their lips parted as though they wanted to speak, but had forgotten how.

"It's simple, but it's gotten complicated," Noah said.

"I told my parents the next day," Rebecca said. The color had not faded from her face. He was pretty sure that under her *Kapp,* her entire scalp was blushing. "And I would have told you all yesterday, except the doctor said we weren't to argue with Andrew. We were to keep him calm, try to guide him to reality, but to play along if we could so we didn't stress him. So you can imagine my feelings when he spoke this morning, and told you all that he —that I—"

"That he thinks you're engaged," Sim said, a little flatly. "I can't believe this."

"Me neither," his youngest sister said.

Poor Clara. She'd been so happy and excited, and now she looked the way she had when she was six, the time she'd fallen out of their pony cart and landed flat on the road, the breath knocked out of her.

"I guess we know now that people can hear when they're sedated," Patricia, the ever practical, said with an air of looking on the bright side.

"That's not the point," Sim told her. "The point is that we believed a lie, and Mamm and Dat still do, and now so does the whole church because *certain people* couldn't keep it to themselves yesterday."

Now, that wasn't fair, Noah thought as Clara pressed her fingers to her mouth. She was a talker. But it was all too late now.

"I'm so sorry," Rebecca said, her voice trembling. "I—I didn't correct the mistake in time, and before I knew it—"

"It was out, like tares blowing over the fence into a wheat field," Sim finished.

"And who knows what mischief we'll be harvesting," Naomi Miller said.

"What are we going to do?" Clara wailed. "Oh, this is so embarrassing."

"How do you think I feel?" Rebecca mumbled, but Noah was pretty sure Clara hadn't heard her.

"We can't deceive the church," Reuben told them in a tone that held thoughtful authority. The van fell silent. "That much is obvious. But we don't have to answer questions, either. We don't have to feed the fire. The baptism is in two weeks, Rebecca, so people will be focused on that. Maybe by then this whole thing will blow over. A nine days' wonder."

"But what about our parents?" Patricia wanted to know. "What do we tell them? We can't leave them in the dark."

"Of course not," Noah said. "We'll tell them the next time they call with news. And stress to them that they need to be careful. Guide Andrew back to reality, but don't argue, like the doctor said."

Sim snorted. "Maybe he'll think the engagement was all a hallucination, too. Along with the bears. And the kitten riding on Rebecca's shoulder."

"And those packs of cigarettes hidden in the ceiling," Patricia added. "That was this morning's vision. Where does his mind collect such things?"

"The medications," Naomi said firmly. "None of it has any relation to reality. Though if I saw Rebecca with a kitten on her shoulder, it would be out in the barn in two seconds."

"If he'd said it was a chicken, I might not have believed he was hallucinating," Reuben said to his subdued daughter with a smile. "Rebecca looks after the hens at the Circle M. Some of them do ride on her shoulder."

And the horses dance ballet? But Noah didn't say that out loud. "So it's agreed, then?" was what he did say. "We tell Mamm and Dat the truth as soon as we can."

"And if people in the church have questions or want to know Rebecca's plans, say it's off," Reuben advised.

"Wunderbaar," Rebecca said with a groan. "They'll think I've dumped a man in his hour of need. I'll not only be a liar, but a cruel one as well."

"Once Andrew realizes it's all a mistake," Naomi said soothingly, "we'll let it be known he has broken up with her. And then it will be done."

"Goodness knows he's had enough practice at that," Clara agreed. "Like that poor girl he threw over. I heard about it when we were in Amity. Anna something."

Anna May Helmuth. She was such a nice person, and Noah had liked her. She was far too good for his brother, and far too nice to have been treated like that.

They passed a sign for the Siksika Valley Neurological Rehabilitation Center, visible in a grove of trees at the end of a long, curving drive. *"Funded by a generous donation from the Madison Family Trust,"* Patricia read as the van sped past.

"That's the family on the Rocking Diamond ranch, up the road from us," Naomi said. "They are *very* well funded."

"I'm glad, if it means we can move Andrew closer," Clara said. "I hope it's not going to be too expensive."

"The church will provide," Reuben told her gently. "And if need be, I might have a word with the Madisons. They may be willing to pull a string or two, once we explain the situation."

Once they drove through Mountain Home, it didn't take long to reach the stripped timber posts holding a crossbeam with the Circle M brand made of wrought iron in the center. The van rumbled up the lane, giving Noah plenty of time to take in the stunning beauty of the place. The ranch house was situated on a knoll overlooking the loops of the Siksika River, just as Rebecca had said. Patches of snow still lay in the shadows from the unpredictable weather that had begun this whole disaster. In the distance, nestled in the trees, was another log house, which Naomi told them would be the home of their eldest son, Daniel, and Lovina Lapp, who would be married at the end of the month.

Three horsemen in the pastures stretching out to the foothills noticed the van and turned for home. Reuben helped his wife down while Rebecca held the baby's carrier, and after a flurry of thanks, Reuben paid the driver and they mounted the steps to the house.

Noah was so overwhelmed by the sheer years of work and good stewardship—the generations of it—it would take to make the Gingerich place prosper like this one that he barely noticed the rest of the trip. As the van crunched into the gravel drive, Noah blinked himself back to the present. Aendi Annie come out on the porch, her shawl wrapped about her against the wind, which was still chilly despite the sunshine.

"I didn't expect you," she said as they climbed out of the van and Simeon paid the driver. "Is Andrew with you? And where are Kate and Arlon?"

After a flood of explanations and news, the taxi van rolled away, and they all trooped inside the *Daadi Haus*. Aendi Annie put coffee on the stove, and sliced what looked like an applesauce cake baked that morning, if the scent in the kitchen was any indication.

"Aendi, we have something else to tell you," Sim said. Noah turned away to put some wood in the woodstove. "Turns out Rebecca Miller isn't engaged to our Andrew after all."

"She's not?" Annie turned from the counter, knife in hand. "What, did he wake up and break it off with her? He can't be in his right senses—you need to tell that dear girl not to despair. It will all turn out right in the end."

"*Neh, Aendi,* that's just it. He did the opposite. She told us there was a misunderstanding at the hospital and the nursing staff thought she was his fiancée. But she's not."

"But when Andrew woke up," Clara chimed in, "he believed it was true."

"So now poor Rebecca thinks she's not engaged to him. But he thinks she is," Patricia went on.

Aendi Annie stared, then put the knife on the counter and bowed her head. Strange sounds came from her pursed lips. Noah and Clara started forward. Had they made her cry? But she tipped her head back and let loose a guffaw of laughter. Leaning on the counter, she laughed until she had to hold her stomach, tears leaking into the fine wrinkles of her face.

"Oh my," she gasped when she could finally speak. "Oh my. What a fine to-do."

"That's just it," Simeon said gloomily. "The news is out in the church, and we can't take it back."

Still chuckling, Annie brought the cake to the table. "Patricia, will you pour the coffee? And Clara, there are sausage rolls in the oven that should be ready. Ah me, I knew that life would be lively once Kate's family arrived in Mountain Home. I will say this for my relatives—there is never a dull moment."

HOWEVER THE NEWS was going over in the Gingerich household, Rebecca thought, it couldn't be worse than the sensation it was making on the Circle M. Baby Deborah's introduction to her family was positively placid compared to this.

"So let me get this straight," Joshua said as they settled around the big kitchen table and Malena and Sara brought over a mountain of sandwiches, as well as two different kinds of cookies—ginger snaps (Rebecca's favorite) and oatmeal chocolate chip (Dat's favorite). He held Nathan in his lap, his incredulous gaze on his older sister. "You're *not* engaged to Andrew King? And you never have been? Then why were the King sisters chattering like magpies about it yesterday after church?"

Unraveling the ins and outs of the story took most of their lunch together.

Malena, for once in her life, was stricken nearly silent.

Nearly. Three ... two ... one ...

"I can't believe it," her twin burst out. "It was a thunderclap to learn that you were engaged to him. But to learn that you're not is like—like—"

"A wet blanket?" Adam suggested.

"Raining on her parade," Zach said, nodding.

"Whose parade—Rebecca's or Malena's?" Adam asked. "I don't know who is more disappointed. Rebecca for not getting married, or Malena, for not being able to gossip about it."

"Boys," Mamm said in the tone that brought them around like a horse being reined into a switchback. "I'm only going to say this once. All this is a mistake. A stone that never should have been thrown into the pond. But now we have to live with the ripples. The important thing to remember here is that your teasing can hurt your sister. She's been through a lot since Friday night. When, I might remind you, she saved a man's life. So when you open your mouth to say something you think is funny, consider for just one second how it will sound in her ears. And her heart."

"*Ja*, Mamm," Andrew and Zach mumbled.

"Malena?" Mamm persisted.

"Me?" Malena's grey eyes, the only feature she shared with her twin, widened. "I didn't say anything."

"Much," Joshua muttered. Baby Nathan waved a hand in the air in agreement.

"Come on, Mamm," Malena wheedled. "Rebecca is so quiet this is practically the first time in our lives we've had the chance to tease her."

"Do you have amnesia, too?" Rebecca blurted, goaded beyond endurance. Every head at the table swung in her direction. Even tiny Deborah blinked. "Have you forgotten all the times I had to hide out in the barn with the chickens? When you wouldn't let me alone with your laughing about some mistake I made?"

Malena looked as though she were gazing into the distant past, trying to locate a memory.

"Did we do that?" Adam nudged Zach.

"Couldn't have been us." Zach shook his head.

"Your sister needs you to stand by her," Dat said, taking the baby from Mamm so that she could finish her lunch. "And that means here on the Circle M as well as out in the district."

"Of course we'll stand by her," Sara Fischer said. "Believe me, I know firsthand the damage that idle gossip can do, not only to the person concerned, but also to everyone around her. That's why I left Mountain Home nearly ten years ago. I couldn't stand it—people remembering the gossip when they looked at me, instead of a grieving kid who didn't know how to atone. That's what drove me away in the end. Knowing I couldn't make headway against what people thought of me. Or at least, what I *thought* they thought of me."

"Rebecca's problem isn't nearly as serious as yours was," Joshua said, taking her hand with his free one. "But let's face it, many of the same people still live here."

"And I have faith that God is dealing with their hearts," Mamm said, her gaze soft on Sara's face. The planes and angles of it had begun to fill out since she'd come to them, Rebecca noticed. And her happiness gave her a kind of radiance that she was pretty sure Joshua fell in love with all over again, every time he looked at her.

Rebecca realized, in the middle of a bite of her sandwich, that this was the evidence of real love. This mutual support, this beauty that each saw in the other, this sense of being settled in the life God had chosen for them—she'd never experienced any of it. In that moment, she saw herself as she really was. A dreamer, trying to make a warm sweater that would last against life's storms out of bits of cloud that only evaporated when she touched them. Dreaming about Andrew, with no support for those dreams at all.

Was that why she'd allowed the misunderstanding to go on before her heart's urging toward truth became too much to ignore? Because she wanted something to happen?

Of course it was.

And now that something had—now that, as Noah said, almost his whole family was being forced to tell her lie—it was time to face the reckoning.

The King siblings would tell Kate and Arlon as soon as they could. They would tell Andrew as soon as his mind was healthy enough to hear it.

But her task was bigger even than that, and had eternal consequences.

She swallowed her bite of sandwich with a gulp. "I have to see Bishop Joe," she said. "The truth has to start with him."

"A good decision, *Dochder*," Reuben said with a slow nod. "You should arrange to take the final baptism class you missed yesterday. That would be a *gut* opportunity."

"I'll go this afternoon."

The prospect of doing something active, of no longer waiting in the shadows for the next bad thing to happen, was almost a relief.

CHAPTER 11

*A*fter a brisk walk of just under a mile, Rebecca turned into the wooded lane on the opposite side of the highway from the Circle M, the home of "Little Joe" Wengerd, their six-foot-five bishop and his wife, Sadie. Along the sides of the lane, the pines were their usual dark green, but among them were more delicate trees like aspens and birches, their bare branches beginning to blush with new life. She found Ruby, the youngest Wengerd daughter, who was unmarried and still at home, alone and folding laundry in the basement. Just like at their place, the clothesline was strung across the room so that the clothes would dry in the heat of the woodstove. Come May, they would hang their laundry outside again, but for now, the prospect of taking in frozen laundry was so unappetizing that most of the women in the district did it this way.

"One of the sure signs of spring," Ruby said with a smile. "Laundry will be outside on the line. How are you? And congratulations. You're the second of our buddy bunch to be engaged, after Sara."

Rebecca's stomach did a barrel roll.

"About that. Is the bishop at home?"

"He's in the barn with a couple of young cows that he figured would have trouble birthing." Ruby's smile illuminated her whole face. "Have you come to set a date for the wedding? Goodness, Rebecca, how could you keep such a secret? I'd have been spreading it far and wide if it were me." Her delight dimmed just a trifle. "Though the likelihood of my having news like that isn't very good. I haven't met the youngest brother, but Susan Bontrager has already set her cap for Simeon King. She says it must be God's will because their names go so well together." She rolled her eyes. "That girl is desperate with a capital D, and if the King boys don't know it now, someone had better tell them."

Rebecca prayed for strength.

"I have come about that. In a way." No, she couldn't do this. No half-truths and evasions. Ruby had been her friend since they were in diapers, and she didn't deserve that disrespect. "The truth is, I'm not engaged. It was all a mistake."

Ruby's hazel eyes widened, and her freckles seemed to stand out in relief against skin that had gone pale. "He broke it off? After you saved his life? How could he? The whole district knows you went in the ambulance with him."

"I should be so lucky. No, it was a mistake at the hospital."

"But—"

"What you just said is true—God used me to help him. But at the hospital, there was a misunderstanding about my relationship to Andrew, and when his family arrived, it got passed on to them. And then the doctor said—" She waved her hands in frustration. "Never mind. The point is, I'm not engaged to him. So I have to tell your father that, and make sure that, despite this *Huddlerei*, I can still be baptized in two weeks."

Ruby stared at her in astonishment. "You're not engaged."

"Neh."

"Then why were his sisters— Only yesterday—"

"They didn't know either, until I told them today on the way home. Mamm and Dat agreed that I should clear it up right away. The problem is, their parents still think I am. And Andrew thinks I am."

Ruby shook her head as though flies were buzzing in her brain. "I thought he was under sedation."

"He came out of it. And there I was, and there his parents were, and oh Ruby, I've made such a colossal mess." Her throat closed and she hugged her friend, who patted her on the back helplessly. "I need to talk to the bishop. I need help."

"Of course. Want me to walk you to the barn?"

"No, I know you have work to do. I'll be all right."

Ruby set her at arms' length. "What's he like? Andrew?"

Rebecca almost laughed, but poor Ruby wouldn't understand what was so funny. Funny in a dark way. "I don't know. Other than talking to him when he was unconscious—because they thought I was his fiancée they let me into the ICU—I've never actually spoken to him."

Those brown eyes searched hers. "You met him in Colorado. Didn't you."

Oh, she was a smart one. Rebecca nodded. "I could say our eyes met across a crowded room, but even that would be a lie. He never noticed me until yesterday, when he came out of the sedation and his parents told him who I was." She amended, "Who they thought I was."

"I knew something had happened out there. I thought it might be a man, but you never said anything."

"If not for that one stupid mistake at the hospital, I still wouldn't have said anything. He wouldn't know I was alive, and I'd just quietly have my little crush, and none of this would be happening."

"Except *he* might not be alive, if not for you," Ruby said. "I hope he's grateful."

"I don't know how much his parents have told him. He's not ... quite right in the head. The drugs. Noah hopes he'll think I'm just another hallucination."

"Noah. That's the youngest brother?"

Rebecca could have smacked herself for bringing him up. *"Ja.* The grumpy one. He doesn't like me very much right now."

"Then he doesn't know you," Ruby said loyally.

But Rebecca didn't want to talk about Noah. "Thanks for letting me tell you about it, Ruby. Now I'd best go find the bishop."

Bishop Joe was just as astounded as his daughter when Rebecca finished her silly and pathetic story. She herself was so embarrassed she could hardly look up. Telling one's best friend was one thing. But telling the bishop—God's chosen shepherd of the church—that she had been so foolish was entirely different.

"Well, I'll be dipped." Little Joe took off his black felt hat and scratched his head all over, as though that would get his brain working again. He leaned on the side of the calving pen, where the exhausted cow he'd been watching had had her calf and was beginning to take an interest in it.

Rebecca leaned on the other side, her arms crossed on the

top metal rail. "I wanted you to know the truth," she concluded. "So you can decide whether or not I'm worthy to be baptized in two weeks."

He looked at her sharply, his prematurely white beard seeming to bristle with surprise. "Why should you not be baptized, child?"

It was what she'd dearly wanted to hear, but she wasn't taking any chances.

"Because I deceived a whole bunch of people. I didn't speak up in time—didn't stop the deception when I could. I let it go on because—" She gulped. "I let it go on. And now the whole district believes a lie, and the ones who don't have to keep telling it for me. Until we know that Andrew King understands the truth."

Little Joe fitted his hat back on his head and considered the calf, who was tottering around the pen, getting used to his legs.

"What does that mean, until Andrew King understands the truth?"

"At the hospital, they're giving him drugs for the swelling in his brain. But they make him hallucinate. He says really strange things as though they're completely real. And one of those things was about us making a life together." She omitted her mistake in saying such a thing when she didn't really believe Andrew could hear. "The problem is, no one knows if he really believes that, or if it's just another hallucination, like the doctors walking bears down the corridor on leashes."

The bishop blinked at her. "He saw that?"

"He did yesterday. So until we know he's in his right mind again, the doctor says we're not to argue with what he says. What he believes. In case it stresses his brain."

"But if Andrew is in Libby, who is there to argue?"

"His parents. They're still with him. Simeon and Noah and their sisters came back with us this afternoon. They're going to get started on the renovations to the farmhouse."

"Glad to hear it. That house deserves a family in it, and Annie needs them with her." But he sounded as though his mind was elsewhere. Then he looked up. "I'm going to need to pray on this. It seems to be more complicated than I thought."

Oh, what a tangled web we weave...

"Especially since the district believes what Andrew and his parents believe," Joe went on. "This is not exactly something I can announce after church."

The faint hope that he might do just that died in Rebecca's heart.

"Can I still take my last baptism class?" she asked faintly.

"Ach, *ja*. I can give it to you right here, if you like. After my years in this position, I've got the Confession memorized, to say nothing of the questions I must ask."

At least that would be a step in the right direction.

So with the tired cow and the curious calf as witnesses, with April mud on her boots, Rebecca received the instruction that her brother and sister and Sara had received yesterday before church. Whether or not God moved the bishop to allow her to be baptized, at least she would be ready should he call her name and include her. She could only pray that she would be with her *Schweschder* and *Bruder* and Sara at the front of the room, feeling the holy water trickling over her head as everything she'd done wrong in the past week—and farther back—was washed away.

That hope must keep her going for the next two weeks.

Because goodness knew things couldn't get much worse.

❦

NOAH GUIDED Annie's horse into the bishop's lane, following the directions his great-aunt had written out for the journey. Simeon had offered to come with him, but he had declined. All he wanted was to be alone during his first foray out into the country that would be his home for the next couple of months. To smell the wet pines as the last of the snow melted off them in the afternoon sun. To see the winter sparrows skip from branch to branch, watching his progress down the lane in Annie's ancient spring wagon. To hear the Canada geese, somewhere far overhead, honking as they returned to the north from the southern climates where they had been all winter.

A smile of quiet happiness had settled on his face as he rounded a curve—which faded into dismay when the horse slowed at the sight of Rebecca Miller. He clamped his lips together on the "What are you doing here?" that wanted to come out, and instead made calming noises to the old gelding, who came to a full, unwilling stop.

"Whoa," Rebecca murmured, putting a hand on his neck and patting it. "It's only me, Rowan. You know me."

Rowan snorted on her black wool coat and appeared to forgive her.

"I wasn't expecting to see you out and about so soon," she said to Noah. "We've only just got back."

"I could say the same."

Her cheeks were flushed, but why, he couldn't tell. Did seeing him embarrass her? If so, that was *gut*. She had a lot to be embarrassed about.

"I was here to ask the bishop about being baptized," she said in a low tone, mostly to Rowan.

She owed neither of them an explanation. All the same, the answer was too important for anyone to ignore. "What did he say?"

"He needs to pray on it. He understands that the situation is ... complicated."

There was an understatement.

"At least he gave me the baptism class I missed yesterday. In the birthing pen. From memory." Noah's eyebrows rose in spite of his determination not to give his thoughts away. "Welcome to Montana," she said with a passable attempt at a smile. "You won't find anyone standing on ceremony around here."

A little silence fell. Instead of flapping the reins over Rowan's back and continuing on his way, Noah found himself wanting to explain why he was there, too. "Aendi Annie says that the bishop has a job lot of plumbing fixtures in the barn that are newer than what she has in the house. She thought I ought to come and look at them before he sells them to someone else."

"Do you want some help loading them?" she asked at once. She flexed her fingers. "I may not look it, but I'm strong."

"You'd have to be, to get my brother into the back of a buggy." Oh, why had he said that? He'd managed not to think of any of that for fifteen whole minutes.

"That was *der Herr*," she told him frankly. "But plain old me ought to be able to manage some faucets and pipes."

Sim had asked the same question and Noah had declined. But now he nodded, and slid the wagon's passenger door open. She hopped up on the worn, cracked seat and he clicked his tongue to the horse.

"It feels good to be home," she said with a sigh, her gaze lifting over the bishop's split-rail fence to the mountains standing guard around the valley. "Funny what a difference forty miles makes. I've been away a total of three days and it feels like weeks."

"There was a lot packed into those three days."

"And not enough sleep," she admitted. "What do you think of our valley?"

"I thought the Wet Mountain Valley was the most beautiful place I'd ever seen. Then I came here." He shook his head.

"My father says that God is good, and the west Kootenai is the proof."

"I won't disagree."

"I never want to leave it," she said, clasping her hands in her lap.

"Not even to get married?" He did not add *to my brother*.

"That's not likely," she said bluntly. "I'll be the spinster daughter with the sensational past. Taking care of my parents and riding fence with the cowhands. Getting wrinkled and weatherbeaten and not caring. Because I'll be here, where I belong."

He glanced at her curiously. "Don't you want to get married?"

"I didn't say I didn't want to. I said it wasn't likely. But I suppose that part is up to God—and a good thing, too. Look at the mess I made when I was on my own. But for now, I'm just going to stay where He's put me. If someone is meant for me, he'll be the kind who stays, too."

He'd met plenty of girls who wanted to get married, but

not many who put life conditions on it. "What if a man is the one God has sent to you, but he's the kind who goes? Who has a life somewhere else? In Colorado, lots of people come for summer work, but only a few stay. It's no place for farming, and if that's what a man does, they tend to leave." He shrugged.

"So far I haven't had to worry about that," she said. "We get lots of summer visitors, too. But not too many see past my sister once they meet her."

"That's hard to believe," came out of his mouth before he could stop it.

"You haven't met my sister," she said dryly.

He pulled up in front of the big log barn's doors, to be met by a giant of a man with a white beard and piercing blue eyes.

"Back so soon?" the giant said.

"Bishop, this is Noah King, the youngest of the King brothers staying at Annie's," Rebecca said, climbing down from the wagon. "I met him in the lane. Noah, this is Joe Wengerd."

"Everyone calls me Little Joe." The two men shook hands, and Joe looped Rowan's leading rein over the fence and took in the spring wagon. This was clearly not a social call. "What can I do for you?"

"Aendi Annie thought I might take a look at that job lot of plumbing parts."

"The Amish grapevine is efficient. I just picked them up on Saturday. Come on in."

It didn't take long for Noah to strike a deal, and then the three of them loaded the spring wagon. The pipes were practically new, and some of the faucets were still in their packaging.

"I got lucky at an estate sale a ways down the valley," Little Joe said with satisfaction. "I'm glad to know all this stuff will go to make Annie more comfortable. She means a lot to us here."

"She means a lot to my mother," Noah said. "Mamm and her siblings lost their folks young, and my aunts and uncles were split up among the family." Again, his gaze was drawn to the mountains, their peaks white and blue with snow. "She was the lucky one, to come here."

Joe chuckled. "The mountains, they get to you, don't they?"

"There are mountains in Colorado, too, but not like this."

"Once they get to us, we're never the same. I predict you'll be making your home here some day. I recognize the signs."

But Noah backed away, shaking his head and trying to smile. The bishop was obviously teasing him. "Not me. My brothers and I are in business together in Amity. We've built a house there. Settled."

But the bishop only smiled as if he knew something Noah didn't, and untied Rowan's rein. "My wife Sadie will be happy to have you all over for dinner sometime soon. Say tomorrow? It's got to be a chore for your mother to rustle up a good supper when your things haven't got here yet. So one of your sisters said to my Ruby yesterday after church."

"That's kind of you, Bishop." He climbed into the buggy. "It's a fact. I think I can speak for my parents when I say we'd be glad to come. Rebecca, if you like, I can give you a lift back to your place."

He hadn't expected such a welcome from the bishop so soon. After Rebecca settled beside him once more, he clicked his tongue to Rowan and they trundled and rattled and clanked their way back up the lane.

"If the folks in the valley are as hospitable and kind as their bishop, it'll be hard to leave in May," he said.

"You're leaving in May?" she said in surprise.

"Didn't you hear me tell the bishop we have a business in Amity? We can't stay indefinitely. Building season starts in late May, when we're pretty sure it's not going to snow again."

"So does spring turnout. I'm sorry you'll miss it."

He was, too. His curiosity about it would just have to go unsatisfied, though.

"You have a lot of work ahead of you between now and then," she went on.

"We're no strangers to work," he said mildly. A deer paused between two trees, then, at the racket they were making as they passed, bounced away.

"Of course not," she agreed. "I just meant it's going to be a lot."

"It would have been less if Andrew had come and got started like he said he would." He hoped he didn't sound as irritated as his brother's irresponsibility made him feel. "But no point crying about it, I guess. We'll just hoe in and do as much as we can."

"Maybe some of the men from around here can help." She straightened. "I know—a work frolic. Maybe on Friday?"

"I'm not going to ask the men to take a day from their own work to do ours," he said. "Not when I don't know any of them."

"But we know all of them," she pointed out. "And I will guarantee that every one will pitch in for Annie's sake." She bit her lip. "Sorry. I didn't mean that the way it sounded."

"I know what you meant." He didn't want to, but he couldn't help thinking that a work party would put them farther ahead in a day than Andrew's goofing around would have put them in a month. This was no time to be proud and stubborn, and insist that he and Sim could do it themselves. "If I put together a punch list, maybe I could bring it over tomorrow, and your dad could take a look at it and put the word out?"

"Sure."

He pulled on a rein and guided the horse toward the big gate of the Circle M.

"Oh, you don't have to take me in, Noah." She was already sliding the door open, and hopped out before he could even bring Rowan to a halt. "Not with all the pipes and things. You need to get those home. See you tomorrow?"

"In the morning," he managed to get out, but she was already through the gate, walking rapidly up the lane.

She turned with a wave, then vanished around the bend.

He clicked to Rowan and got back on the wide shoulder of the highway. If he didn't know better, he'd almost wonder if she didn't want him to meet her brothers and sisters.

But that was silly. He'd meet them tomorrow, and in church for the next several meetings. He was already looking forward to seeing the inside of that house. And to seeing Reuben and Naomi again.

CHAPTER 12

*M*oah's business was with Dat, Rebecca thought with some relief the next morning. There was no need for them to run into one another as they had yesterday, no need to feel again that complete embarrassment that seemed to wash over her whenever she saw him. And if he did come into the house, she would simply stay in the sewing room and work on the wedding quilt until he was gone.

At nine o'clock, Annie Gingerich's ancient spring wagon rattled up the lane. From the front windows, Rebecca saw it pass the house and draw up in front of the barn. Dat came out, removing his work gloves, and both Noah and his brother Simeon got down and shook hands.

She took a deep breath as they disappeared into the barn, and got busy with the dry mop on the gleaming planks of the living-room floor.

"Who's that?" Malena called from the kitchen, where she and Sara were making German chocolate pies.

"The King brothers," Rebecca said, mopping closer to the archway so she could talk without shouting. "Noah wanted to talk with Dat about maybe having a work day at Annie's on Friday."

"How do you know?" Malena's raised eyebrows sent the heat into Rebecca's face. "Why are you blushing?"

"Some people just do," Sara said, coming to her rescue. "Are those pecans ready?"

Malena gave the plastic bag of pecan halves a couple of extra whacks with the rolling pin to finish breaking them in pieces, then poured them into the coconut.

Rebecca said, "I mentioned it to him yesterday. We ran into each other in the bishop's lane."

"It's a *gut* idea," Sara got in before Malena could say a word about how secretive Rebecca was these days. "Best to get the house repaired as far as possible, and then Kate and the girls still have time to get the garden in." Sara had gardens on the brain now that her own house was fixed up inside and the weather had improved enough to think about the yard and property. "We're going to be swimming in produce by August, aren't we, with two gardens producing. But at least Mamm's— I mean, *our* pantry will be full by the time we're married, with all the canning and drying I plan to do."

"It will be a *gut* start to your lives together," Malena agreed. "Though the thought of my baby brother as a husband and father still makes me feel old. And a little *verhuddelt*."

"Yes, you're so old," Sara teased. "Rattle your creaky bones over here with those nuts. This chocolate mixture is ready."

"A work party," Malena said, combining the ingredients. "There will be work for the women, too, just like there was at your house, Sara."

"Dat will tell us," Rebecca predicted. "Noah wanted to go over the punch list with him."

"You sound like such a carpenter," Malena teased. "Punch list. You and Noah must be doing a lot of talking."

Rebecca shook her head. "I've known him a grand total of three days, and for half that time he thought I was engaged to his brother."

"Well, put like that..." Faced with facts, her twin subsided.

Rebecca dared to hope that Mamm's lecture at lunch yesterday might have done some good.

The pies went into the oven and she finished up her mopping of the living room and the hallways. Beat the hallway runners over the deck rail. Swept the kitchen once the bakers had done the dishes.

And still the King brothers and Dat stayed in the barn. How long did it take to go over a list of jobs and figure out which of the men in the district might do what?

At which point Rebecca gave herself a little talking-to. Their business was none of hers. Her business, now that the housework was done, was to work on the quilt that she, Sara, and Malena were making as a wedding gift for Daniel and Lovina. Ruby and Sadie Wengerd were giving the couple the Flying Geese quilt that Malena had helped to design, and which they'd finished just after Christmas. But upstairs was one of Malena's original designs, straight out of her brain, from scratch.

That her sister possessed this talent still amazed Rebecca. She herself had received no gifts along that line. She could make neat stitches, nine to the inch, and she enjoyed piecing and quilting, but the ability to see a finished design in her head and then do the arithmetic that it took to create it was a gift that *der Herr* alone had bestowed on her twin.

This one was a combination of Double Wedding Ring and

Flying Geese, since they now knew that the latter was one of Lovina's favorite patterns. The geese triangles flew in and out of the rings, their traditional Amish colors changing from the greens and yellows of spring and summer to the burgundy and brown of autumn, to the purple and pale blue of winter, all on a field of wedding-dress blue that would wear well. All that was left to do now was the quilting in the last border, with its scrolling feathers, and then the binding. The wedding wasn't far away now, she reminded herself as she settled in front of the quilt frame, so there was no time to lose.

When some time later she heard the sounds of the table being set for lunch downstairs, Rebecca was certain Noah would have gone ages ago. So it was a shock when he came in with her brothers, all talking a mile a minute.

He glanced at her as he took off his coat and hat, and—argh!—of course she blushed. What was the matter with her? She did her best to fade into the background, which normally was pretty easy when Malena was in the room.

But not this time.

It sounded as though Dat had been on the phone, and word had gone out about the work party. Joshua, Simeon, and Dat were deep in a discussion about water pipes, but Noah was completely absorbed by Adam and Zach's tales of "working" the yearling calves, branding and tagging them, and giving them their vaccinations and worm medicine. The ranchers in the valley helped each other out on those days, both owners and cowhands pitching in, then enjoying a massive meal afterward at the host ranch. Rebecca wished Daniel were here to tell Noah about trailing the mothers and calves and yearlings up into the grazing allotments for the summer, and every possible way things could go wrong—or wonderfully right.

They were expecting Daniel any day, coming with Lovina and Joel to put the finishing touches on their home before the wedding.

At least three times during the meal, which was rich with stories and laughter, Rebecca caught Noah's eye. So much for trying to fade into the woodwork. What did he want from her? And why did what he wanted concern her? As soon as the dishes were done, she promised herself, she was going back up to the sewing room and staying there until she heard their buggy drive away.

"You boys," Mamm laughed as Sara cut the German chocolate pie and Rebecca made a fresh pot of coffee. "You talk as if you're trying to convince Noah to stay for spring turnout."

"He can ride," Adam pointed out. "And if he and Sim stay for just a couple of weeks extra, that's two hands to help and we can tell the Madisons no when they offer."

"I don't think they want to give up two weeks of their own work to disoblige the Madisons," Malena said. "Besides, we owe the Rocking Diamond a lot."

"Not after they tried to snake Sara's hay farm out from under her," Zach said.

"They did what?" Noah said, his fork suspended over his pie.

"He exaggerates," Sara told him. "They made me an offer they thought I couldn't refuse. But they had an ulterior motive, and fortunately, we found out in time what it was."

"You wouldn't have sold to them anyway," Rebecca said. "Not your family's farm. Joshua's and your future home."

"Of course not." Sara smiled over little Nathan's head at

Joshua, who seemed to feel it, for he left off his discussion to smile back.

What a change love had made in her youngest brother. Rebecca couldn't help but marvel at it. Gone was the rocky temper, the dissatisfied, downturned mouth, the gaze that was always on the horizon seeking a way of escape. Now his gaze was clear and full of love, and focused on his son and bride-to-be. On making a home for them—one their church family could meet in after they were married. Every couple establishing a new home made certain it was built in a way that would hold the body of believers in their district. Of course, Sara's family home already did, but Daniel had built his house with that in mind—a big living room overlooking the river, bedrooms enough for the children they hoped to have together, and a kitchen that could feed both guests and family alike.

"I have to admit," Noah confessed, "staying for spring turnout is sure tempting."

Simeon finally turned from the discussion of pipes and water pressure. "Staying for what?"

Joshua quickly explained what the term meant.

"Tempting, maybe, but not possible," Simeon said, shaking his head firmly. "As it is, we'll have to work on Annie's house from sunup to sunset, straight through for a month if Mamm and the girls are to move in before we go."

"I know," Noah said.

Rebecca figured he might have said more, but then thought better of it.

"I want to be back in Amity as soon after May fifteenth as we can," Simeon went on. "I've already had a couple of inquiries about our availability, and don't forget we have Joshua and Amanda King's house to build."

"I haven't forgotten," Noah said. "But a couple of weeks won't make much difference to that project. Joshua has already got all his permits and had the well dug this month. He's already ahead."

"All the more reason for us to start," Simeon said. "The point is, we need to be available to customers who want even small jobs once the weather clears up. Every bit helps toward our own mortgage."

"*Ja*, Sim, I know."

"Then what?" Simeon's brows met in a puzzled frown. "Why this talk about spring turnout when you know you aren't able to help?"

"Just dreaming, I guess," Noah said mildly.

Rebecca had to admire him for not allowing himself to get into an argument when they were guests in someone else's home. At the same time, surely a couple of weeks wouldn't make much difference in Amity when Noah could be useful here in Mountain Home and every hand was a blessing?

"Rebecca," Dat said, "Noah here was interested in some of the detail work our Daniel is doing in his house. Maybe you'd show him the way over there while Simeon and I talk about organizing his crews."

"I—well, I was going to—" Rebecca stammered.

"I can take him," Malena said. "I've been inside all day."

"*Neh, Dochder,*" Mamm told her. "Deborah is down for her nap, so you and I can finish up the quilting. Didn't you say you wanted your gift finished and in its box with a bow on it by the time Daniel comes home? That will be any time now."

Malena had the sense not to argue with their mother. For

one thing, she *had* said that. And for another, she'd only met Noah an hour ago. What would they have to talk about?

Rebecca was already wondering that herself, as she put on her coat and boots. Adam and Zach could have taken him, and regaled him with even more tales of ranch life, but they had work to do on the not-so-romantic side of that life, namely cleaning calving pens and mucking out the horses' stalls.

Well, she could talk about spring turnout as well as they could. If worse came to worst, she could always tell him how to give an unwilling calf a shot.

They set out on the muddy cut that would be a driveway soon, looping below Mamm and Dat's house and curving around the bowl the river had carved over the years. Daniel and Lovina's house perched on a point of land, with a stand of poplars to give it privacy and the shoulder of the mountain behind them to shelter it from the north wind.

"*Dei Bruder* chose his location well," Noah remarked as they approached the house.

"Dat and he have gone in as full partners on the ranch, so it seemed reasonable he should have his own home here," Rebecca said as she let them into the mudroom off the kitchen and took off her boots. "That was before Lovina came back into his life. They're being married here on the twenty-ninth. He's been out in Whinburg Township with her and her son Joel, wrapping up her life there and selling her house and business."

"Sounds like a big job."

"I suppose it is. But her letters are so happy and funny. They seem to find a way to see the bright side of things, even when it's a lot of work."

"I wish Sim could do the same," Noah said unexpectedly. "I

don't know why he's so set on our going back on some exact date he's decided. What difference does a couple of weeks make? I would really like to lend a hand with the branding and spring turnout."

For about a second, Rebecca debated whether to speak. And then her mouth opened without her brain's permission.

"I think Andrew's accident has affected him more than we know," she said. "Maybe he believes he doesn't have authority over Andrew, and he does over you. Maybe he's just trying to control what he can, to make up for what he can't control."

Noah stared at her.

She expected him to say something like, *What do you know about it?* Or *How dare you make assumptions about my brother?*

Instead, he said, "And there you have my brother's personality in a nutshell."

She wasn't sure whether or not she ought to apologize for her forwardness. "Daniel and Joshua have a close bond, but I used to see some of the same feelings between the two of them. Daniel would want to warn Joshua about his wildness, and it would only drive Josh away. But Daniel was saying those things out of love. To try to keep him safe."

"I don't think Sim is making me go back to Amity out of love." Noah stood in the kitchen, its shining plank floors cold under their feet. "I like the cabinets. Maple?"

"Ja." The subject of brothers was obviously concluded. "One of our people is a cabinet maker. He does furniture, too, bedframes and dressers and such."

"Your father said I ought to look particularly at the living room windows, and the barn." She led him into the other room, and he took in the windows. "I see. Our people typically don't make them like that. They like them smaller, to keep the heat in."

Instead of one picture window, Daniel had chosen to install tall but narrow windows side by side, with sturdy wood-trimmed posts between. The view was just as lovely, and the windows served to make the room seem cozy rather than open to the elements like a picture window would.

"Dual paned?"

"*Ja,* for sure and certain. You need that here."

"Reuben is clearly thinking of the view out Annie's front room. And her single paned picture window."

"Maybe," she allowed with a smile. "I think nearly everyone in the valley can claim some kind of view. But Dat likes Annie's because of the fields, and the mountains rising behind them. It's lovely in summer. When the hay is about to be cut, and the wild roses are in bloom along the fences."

She rolled her upper lip between her teeth to stop herself from babbling.

"Sounds like someone else likes that view, too."

"We haven't had church there in a few years, but *ja,* I used to like it. I hope your parents will, too, once the place is planted and running properly again."

"That's what I want," he muttered, walking away to examine the windows' woodwork, gleaming with varnish and representing hours of Daniel's labor with sandpaper and brush.

Did he mean, he wanted to see his parents' new home working again? Or that he wanted to be the one working it?

Nothing ventured, nothing gained. She couldn't sink any lower in his estimation, could she? So she asked him.

He stood with his back to her, his gaze on the view

Daniel's family would have as they grew up. She'd begun to think he meant to ignore her nosiness, when he said, "Both. I want both. I want to at least try the ranch life. Learn everything. Do something besides put huge windows in rich people's homes that they only live in for three months out of the year."

"I thought you built homes for our people," she said in surprise.

"We do. But some of those inquiries Sim was talking about? One is about a hunting cabin that has to be two thousand square feet. It's a renovation. And the other is a horse barn for a man who breeds show Percherons. He wants to branch out to those trotting horses or something."

"Oh," she said. "I can see now why Sim wants to keep to a schedule. It's not just fixing up somebody's deck, then."

"There's that, too. But he could go ahead and do the renovation himself. By the time he was ready to build the barn, I'd be back and I would have been able to try my hand at being an Amish cowboy."

"Speaking of barns." She indicated he should put his boots back on and follow her. Across a grassy field was the new horse barn. She opened the people-sized door next to the big sliding carriage door, and pointed upward.

"Ah," he said. "Mortise and tenon." His voice held admiration. "And peeled-log beams holding up the hayloft."

"A loft big enough to hold a wedding," she said with a smile, "though his and Lovina's will be at our house. But his own children might have a wedding or two here someday, or church. He's made it possible for them to do that, at least. Meanwhile, there is room for all the hay his animals will need over winter."

"Does Reuben think Annie ought to have a barn like this?"

"Well, let's just say that hers is going to fall down and squash her old buggy flat before too many more winters pass."

"That's not a project for the next four weeks, though."

"Neh, probably not," she agreed.

He climbed the steep staircase made of short lengths of half logs, and the smell of pine wafted around them when she followed him and emerged at the top. There was still sawdust in the corners from when the carpenters had cleared out their tools.

"Can I ask you a question?" Noah turned to her, his eyes somber.

From the look of him, she wasn't sure she wanted him to. But she couldn't very well say so. *"Ja,* of course."

"What are you going to do if my brother keeps believing you're his intended?"

She had not been expecting *that.* "I— Well, my hope is that he'll come to himself and think it was all a hallucination, like the bears."

"And if he doesn't? If he thinks it's real?"

"In my sister's opinion, you and your family should convince him to break it off. But once again, that's bringing a whole lot of people into it who don't need to be. I've made up my mind that if I have to, I'll *break it off* myself." She made finger quotes around the words, then turned to look out over the empty space below, where there would soon be calving pens and a poultry aviary and a place to put up the buggies. "It feels strange to say that, when there was never anything there to begin with."

"That's been bothering me," he said. "How did it all get started?"

"I told you. I said some silly thing in the heat of the moment, with the ambulance and everyone running around, and the nurse misunderstood and suddenly they were letting me into the ICU with him because they thought I was his fiancée. And I didn't correct them because I *wanted* to be there. I was worried sick about him, though I hardly knew him."

He nodded, absently touching a rafter joint with its oak peg. "Not at all?"

"I knew him to see him. We were at singing together, and church, when I was in Amity." It was humiliating to say it, but she couldn't lie. Not to Noah. "He never took any notice of me. This whole thing is beyond belief. You see, I've never actually spoken to him—when he was conscious."

She saw the moment when he understood. Their entire relationship had been all in her mind, and now somehow it was all in Andrew's mind, and wasn't that completely ridiculous and sad?

It took a moment before he could speak. "Well, if it has to be anyone with us in this mess, I'm glad it's you and not the *Englisch* girl we were afraid of."

"Oh, I think there is an *Englisch* girl," she said, trying not to let *I'm glad it's you* echo in her brain. "Somewhere. Long gone, probably."

Now she had his full attention. "What do you mean?"

"Just that when they went past me on the road that night, the car windows were open and the driver was screaming at him, like they were having an awful fight. I'm pretty sure it was a woman. Then they hit black ice and he must have been so drunk he was trying to get out of the car while it was spinning. He was thrown out the door and went over the bank."

"And what did this woman do?" He looked so horrified that she realized that while the memory was vivid in her own mind, she hadn't really shared it in this much detail with anyone else.

"She took off. Crossed the bridge way too fast, zoomed up the hill, and was gone in about five seconds. I thought at first she'd thrown out a suitcase, or a dog. That's why I went down the bank. To see if it was a dog, and if I could do something for it."

"And you found my brother."

"I didn't know it was him," she confessed. "It was dark. I didn't recognize him until I got to the fire station, and saw him in the electric lights."

"Is that why they sent you with him?"

She nodded. "Because I could identify him. He didn't have any ID on him."

Noah gave a sigh that seemed to come up from his knees. "Because he was living Amish, and had thrown his driver's license in the stove."

"But if he was living Amish, why was he with this *Englisch* girl and not doing the renovations at Annie's like he was supposed to?"

He crossed the loft and descended the stairs. Wordlessly, she followed, wondering if he was going to answer her.

At the barn door, he spoke at last. "I don't know. I guess that's one of the questions we'll have to ask him once he's in his right mind." He paused. "Maybe that's your reason to break up with him. This *Englisch* girl."

"He can't possibly care about her. He could have *died*," she said. "She drove away and just left him there, down the bank in the dark, with the temperature dropping below freezing."

She still couldn't understand it. A person could be angry enough to scream at someone. To drive away without them, even. But not to leave them at the mercy of the elements on a freezing night. To never even look back.

They went out, and Noah closed the door behind them. On the wind, she could smell the pines and the tang of balsam and softening ground. The smell of spring.

But it seemed that they had run out of conversation even about that, because they were both silent on the unfinished road that took them home.

CHAPTER 13

Three days later, before the sun had crested the mountain peaks but the sky was filled with light enough to see, buggies began to roll into Annie Gingerich's yard. Among the first were that of the bishop and both the family buggy and spring wagon of the Millers from the Circle M.

Noah could hardly believe that the men and women of the district, who had barely met them, would respond like this to a call for help with hardly any notice. Or maybe, he thought humbly, it had nothing to do with the Kings at all, and everything to do with how well the Miller family were regarded in the Siksika Valley. But, as Rebecca had pointed out, it was most likely because they loved Annie Gingerich and wanted to see her back in her home. No matter why people had come, he and his family could only be grateful.

He'd spent the last three days since Rebecca's confession out in the barn alternately trying not to think about it, and thinking about nothing else. For all intents and purposes, she was engaged … to a man she'd never even spoken to. Who would believe that?

But it was done, and she was prepared to undo it. And once she did, he had no doubt that she would be the center of such a storm of gossip as this beautiful valley had never seen.

Some might say she deserved it. But in his mind, better that than being engaged to Andrew. He was a lovable enough man on a good day—only those had been in short supply. The battle in his heart to live Amish or live *Englisch* had made him into two men, and a woman as gentle and pretty as Rebecca didn't deserve a man with a divided heart.

And that wasn't even counting this *Englisch* mystery woman who had left him for dead.

"Come on, *Bruder*, time to get to work." Simeon clapped him on the back and Noah lurched into motion, abandoning his thoughts and fastening his leather carpenter's belt about his hips, automatically making certain all his tools were in their places.

Simeon and Reuben Miller acted as foremen, dividing the volunteers into work crews. The old farmhouse had been emptied, the furniture moved out to the barn for the time being. Noah knew that in general, the floors of the house were pretty solid, made of oak planks darkened with time, and a good subfloor under them. But under the fifty-year-old linoleum of the kitchen, there had been some water damage from burst pipes and an old sink. A crew was formed to pull up and replace the flooring, and another to crawl under the house with headlamps to get started replacing the plumbing.

A third crew got busy on the soft spots on the wraparound porch that had so delighted his mother and sisters. Supports would have to be replaced as well as a few planks. The fourth crew focused on the walls, pulling off the old wallpaper-covered plywood and fitting bats of insulation between the studs before replacing it with new drywall. This house was going to be both snug in the winter and cool in the summer, since he and Sim also planned to insulate the attic after they'd replaced the roof, and the ceiling of the basement, once the plumbing was back in operation.

The little *Daadi Haus* where Aendi Annie lived was a hive of activity as well. She, Patricia, and Clara had barely got the breakfast dishes washed and dried before they'd begun on the midday meal for the crew. Noah knew that they expected the women of the community to begin arriving around eleven, bringing covered dishes and bowls to contribute to the meal. They would have to set it out on boards laid across saw horses in the yard, he thought with a smile. With all the drywall dust and missing planks, it wouldn't be safe to go inside the farmhouse until day's end.

"I thought your sisters might have joined you," he said casually to Zach Miller as he followed him upstairs. They'd been assigned to walls, along with a young man he'd been told was the local blacksmith and farrier.

"Not this time," Zach said cheerfully. "But Annie gave them the measurements of every window in the house. They're sewing up insulated curtains today. And Malena is making window quilts for the bedrooms."

"What is a window quilt?" Noah had never heard of such a thing.

"It's a covering for the inside of the window in winter," Alden Stolzfus said, as a sheet of old plywood yielded to his claw hammer with a screech. "Keeps the cold out. Are you putting in dual pane windows in here, Noah?"

"*Ja*," he said. "An outfit out of Libby delivered them three weeks ago, Annie says, so she had them stack them in the barn."

"Soon as we get this plywood out of here, we'll go get them," Zach said. "Windows, insulation, then drywall. Might need some more hands."

More hands arrived. It was like a miracle, how fast the work went when there were so many willing backs to bear the load. It would have taken him and Sim a week just to get the old plywood off the walls.

"We're never going to be able to repay them," he muttered to Simeon as they were washing their hands and faces before lunch. "Not when we're leaving."

"But Mamm and Dat will," Sim assured him. "The girls, too. They'll be first in line to help their neighbors if they're needed, you know they will."

But he wouldn't be here to help. He'd be back in Colorado, working on that barn for trotting horses, probably unable to keep his eyes from looking west past the sunset and wondering if she—if the people here were watching it, too.

He would not waste valuable minutes of this day looking out the new windows, watching for a buggy that was certainly not coming. The Miller and Wengerd women were busy with their sewing bee, doing their part even as he did his.

Which was why it came as a complete surprise to walk outside, slapping drywall dust off the sleeves of his shirt, and find Rebecca and Malena crossing the yard with casserole dishes in their hands. Trestles were already set up, and they set their dishes among the feast that had already been prepared.

The crews gathered around, as did the women who had

brought food, while Little Joe gave thanks for the lunch, for the hands who had served them, and the *gut Gott* who watched over them all as they helped one another.

Noah carried his plate over to where Patricia was eating with the Miller twins, balancing their plates on the top rail of the garden fence. They all ate standing up—there wasn't much point in getting comfortable when there was so much work still to be done. Luckily the sun and hard work combined to make a jacket unnecessary for him, at least. The girls wore black knitted cardigans over work dresses of green and purple and burgundy.

"I wasn't expecting to see the sewing circle over here," he said by way of greeting.

"We made our favorite sausage surprise casserole," Malena told him. "It would be a shame if you couldn't eat it, so we thought we'd share."

"Mamm is home with the babies," Rebecca said. "As soon as we clean up, we're going back. We have a few rooms yet to do, but at least the bedrooms will have new curtains."

"I've finished window quilts for the ones on the north side," Malena said. "Those are needed first. I'll keep working on the rest this week. What a lot of sewing to get done all at the same time! Between the wedding quilt and these, I don't seem to have scheduled myself very well."

"I guess sewing takes more time than knocking out walls," he conceded. "But both of us still have to cut our materials and piece them together."

She laughed at the thought, and Rebecca smiled, too, the dimple in her left cheek making his breath stop just for a second, until he remembered where he was and that Patricia was looking at him far too curiously for his own good.

Simeon ambled up, clearly already on his second plate of food. "Going pretty well, ain't so?"

Which was as close as Sim got to shouting hallelujah.

Noah was about to reply in the affirmative when the girl from the café in Mountain Home—what was her name?—joined their little circle.

"Hallo, Susan," Rebecca said. "Did you close the café to come today?"

"*Neh*, couldn't do that," the girl replied. "It's Friday, and we're learning that Fridays are always busy. I can't stay long. Mamm sent me over with hot dogs and fried onions in a warming tray." She glanced at Simeon's plate. "Glad you're enjoying them."

Sim, whose mouth was full of hot dog, could only nod.

"Any news of your brother Andrew?" Susan said to Sim, as though his mouth wasn't full and Noah wasn't standing right across from her.

Sim gave a mighty swallow. "We heard last night. Mamm called to say that he was going to be moved up here to that rehab facility we saw when we came home." His gaze moved to Rebecca. "That your father's doing?"

Rebecca shrugged, her cheeks blooming with color. "He might have had a little word with Brock Madison. He's the owner of the Rocking Diamond. They lost their eldest boy after a car accident years ago. He had pretty severe neurological problems from it, and didn't live much past twelve. They helped found that clinic in his memory."

"Well, whatever he said, we're grateful," Sim went on. "They're calling it a grant, but what it boils down to is that Andrew is getting his care at a discount."

"Isn't it *wunderbaar?*" Clara beamed. "We owe the church so much."

Noah could only hope that when Andrew learned of what people had given and sacrificed so that he could get well, he would be grateful. And more, that gratitude to the church would lead to gratitude for God, and a change of heart for good and ever.

"His being moved up here will make things easier for you, won't it, Rebecca?" Susan turned her bright blue gaze on her like a searchlight. "You'll be able to visit every day, if you want to." She corrected herself. "Of course you'd want to. He's your fiancé, though I can still hardly believe you could keep such a secret from all your friends."

"Ja," Rebecca managed. It came out like a rasp.

"I suppose it's difficult to make wedding plans when he's laid up," Susan went on while an uncomfortable silence seemed to cover them all like a blanket. "But I'm sure he'll be well soon, and back here with all of you." She made a movement with her hand to indicate a family circle, and her fingers brushed Simeon's sleeve.

He jumped as though a bee had landed on him.

"I go into town every day," she told him. "If you'd like to visit, you just tell me and I'll give you a ride to the clinic."

"I—we—Annie has given us the use of her buggy until ours gets here," Sim said bluntly.

Horribly awkward as this was, Noah thought, better she flirt with Simeon than talk about Andrew with Rebecca.

"Oh, that's good." Susan turned back to Rebecca. "This is the first I've been able to talk with you. I want to know all about it— how you got engaged, where you were, what he said, everything."

Again, scarlet washed up into the roots of Rebecca's hair. Her mouth opened and closed.

"Some things are private," Simeon said, for once noticing something other than nails and siding. "Clara, Dat said you'd mentioned built-in bookshelves in the living room. Can you show me where you want them?"

"Ooh, I want to see," Susan exclaimed.

"Come along, then."

Noah had to admire his brother's sacrifice as the trio took their plates to the dishwashing crew and then went inside. "That was a rescue if ever I saw one."

"He'll be sorry," Malena predicted. "Give that girl a minute, and she'll take the rest of his life."

"She might only get a month. Sim is determined to go back to Amity," Noah told them. "I think he's safe."

The twins looked at one another doubtfully.

As he went back to work, he made a note to himself to warn Simeon not to attract too much feminine attention, if he was bound to return to Colorado. But ... what would their lives be like if they stayed? To wake up every day to the mountains' eternal watch over them. To establish a carpentry business here. A life here.

Neh, the truth was that if he were a carpenter here, he'd be like Andrew, forever torn between what he wanted to do and what he had to do out of obligation to his brother. Sim couldn't run the business alone. It was a load trying to run it with two men. Three had been ideal. But Noah had a feeling that the three King brothers working together had been a brief, shining moment, now relegated to the past. Frankly, with the tangle that Andrew's life had become while he was unconscious in his bed, Noah couldn't see that moment returning.

By nightfall, the old farmhouse had been resurrected and become a completely new home. The plumbing project had been completed—kitchen, bathroom, and laundry sinks in the basement—and the floors replaced in the kitchen. New linoleum hadn't gone down yet, but compared to the work that had been accomplished that day, doing that would be a walk in a summer field. Clara's bookshelves were only a pencil sketch in Simeon's notebook as yet, but it wouldn't take long for them to tape and texture the walls. Once they were painted, they could install the shelving.

Noah looked forward to the sewing circle bringing the curtains and window quilts now that the new windows were in.

"This house feels warmer already," Patricia remarked, walking from one room to the next. "It's amazing what a difference the windows make."

"When we get the new roof on, you'll notice an even bigger difference," Sim told her. "By the time Noah and I go back to Amity, I want to see you moved in, and Aendi Annie comfortable in the downstairs bedroom, where she can be looked after."

"I want that, too," Patricia said. "But do you really have to go back? Why not move the carpentry business here, Sim?"

Noah's heart nearly stopped. He hadn't realized his sister's thoughts had been galloping down the same trail as his own.

"Because we have good prospects in Amity," Simeon told her in a tone that made Noah think maybe he didn't like his little sister's nose in his business. "Isn't that right, Noah?"

"I think we'd have good prospects in any Amish community," he said diplomatically. If there was even a whisper of hope, he wanted Sim to know he was open to it.

"*Ja*, but I'm not only thinking of Amish customers," Sim said. "I'm thinking of *Englisch* customers, and some of those folks out in Colorado have money enough to give us a good living."

"There is more to life than money, Simeon King," Clara told him, coming into the empty kitchen on the tail end of his words. "Mamm and Dat would love it if you settled here, near us. And I have to say I'd love it, too. Having you and Noah twenty hours away means we won't see you for Christmas or family events, unless we were lucky enough to have a mild winter."

"You will if we plan it," Sim said patiently. "Regardless of weather, the train still runs."

"And what about Andrew?" Patricia wanted to know. "When he gets well, is he going back to Amity, too?"

"It's impossible to know, Pat," Noah said when Sim turned away to fiddle with the faucets. "He may be just fine, or he may never work again. If he's going to that neurological clinic, it's more than his fractured leg that's the problem. It means there's something hurt in his brain, too."

She nodded. "That's what Mamm said. When they tried to get him to walk down the hallway, they discovered he's forgotten how on one side. The opposite side from the leg with the cast."

This was news. Noah exchanged a glance of concern with Simeon.

"Do they think it might be permanent?" his brother asked.

"I don't know," Patricia said. "I guess we'll find out. They're sending him up on Monday, so it's *gut* we had the work day today."

It was by sheer chance they'd had the work day today, and even then only because Rebecca had suggested it.

"Does anybody else know he's coming up Monday?" he asked his sister.

"It isn't a secret." She shrugged. "I told some people, and I think Clara did, too. Mostly because they were asking when Mamm and Dat were coming home."

Rebecca couldn't have known on Tuesday, then, when they'd been talking about it. And the little knot in his gut that wondered if she and Andrew were still in touch, loosened.

Of course they weren't talking on the phone. He was being silly.

CHAPTER 14

*A*mong the Amish in the Siksika Valley, off Sundays were quiet days, spent with the family. If the weather was cold, they would read aloud or build puzzles, or write letters, as Mamm and Adam often did. Rebecca and Malena had finished Daniel and Lovina's wedding quilt yesterday, the two of them working together since most of Friday had been devoted to the work party at Annie's.

"I suppose we'll have to start calling it the King place," Malena said as she'd stitched down the final mitered corner of the binding.

"I expect Annie will deed the farm over to Kate and Arlon outright," Mamm had said, rocking Deborah contentedly after her feeding. "They're her heirs, so they would have come into it anyway when she passed."

With his parents living in the valley permanently, then, would they see Noah once or twice a year? And what difference did it make to her? Rebecca asked herself crossly.

It was the knowledge that Andrew was being moved to the valley tomorrow that was making her jumpy. Spoiling her

Sunday, which was usually a sweet day of rest for the family, outside of meal preparation and the necessary animal care. She ought to go for a walk, and put this nervous energy to use.

She leaned in to Joshua's bedroom, where Sara was changing Nathan, and told her where she was going, then pulled on her coat and boots. It was sunny out, but that meant nothing in the mountains, where the weather could change between one breath and the next. She headed past the barn and the corrals to the track that led up the hill to Mammi's orchard. From here, she could look down over the water meadows and the lazy loops of the river. The ice in the shady curves had melted in the last few days of sunshine.

And look! She turned from the view to examine the bright yellow of a cluster of glacier lilies beside the muddy path. "Spring arrived when we weren't looking," she told them. "I'm very glad to see you."

The lilies waved in the breeze. They looked so delicate, but they were hardy little things, sometimes even poking up through the snow. It wouldn't be long now until the other flowers joined them—the pink shooting stars, the cheerful yellow daisy-like flowers of the arrowleaf balsamroot. Up on the hills above the house you could even find the waxy pink blooms of the bitterroot, but that wouldn't be until later, when Mammi's apple trees bloomed.

The track made a zigzag, then led up to the mouth of the box canyon. Even in winter, it always seemed warmer in here to Rebecca, as though the rock walls and rolling grass held it in for the benefit of the trees Dat's mother had planted.

Sure enough, along the knobbly, lichened branches, life was stirring. "It won't be long now," she told the McIntosh.

"I'd better come up here more often, or I'll miss your blossoms altogether. Though I can smell them sometimes, when the wind is just right."

"Who are you talking to?" came an amused voice.

Rebecca whirled to see Noah King standing in the canyon's mouth.

"I feel like I should ask permission to come in," he said.

It was a bit like a room with an open roof, and she was alone in it. But she never felt lonely. Not anywhere on the Circle M.

"What are you doing here?" Oh dear. That sounded rude.

"My parents came home today, since Andrew is being moved tomorrow," he said, strolling closer. He wore gumboots like she did, and a black wool coat, like she did, unbuttoned down the front.

"That's *wunderbaar*, but it makes no answer."

"They've come over to thank your father for the work frolic." He chuckled. "My mother is overwhelmed. I thought she might actually kiss the drywall when she saw all the progress we made."

"It does look completely different now," she agreed, "and that was only what I saw before we went home."

He told her how much had been completed, and how it had nearly brought his mother to tears. "Which is why we came to visit. She just had to thank your parents. In all the racket of five conversations at once, someone mentioned that you were up here."

Sara. Had she gone further, and suggested he come and find her? Her future sister-in-law had better not be getting a little idea about things she shouldn't.

"Do they want me to come back?" she asked. "I'm not sure

I'm able to face your parents." Then another thought struck. "You don't suppose anyone will tell them, do you? That Andrew and I aren't—"

He looked up into the branches of the Goodland. "I'm sure someone will. But honestly, it's for the best. I feel terrible that they're the last to know."

"Except for the church."

"*Ja.* Like that Susan Bontrager, on Friday. It was all I could do not to tell her the truth."

"Perhaps we should have," Rebecca said ruefully. "It would have been all over the district by suppertime, and saved us the trouble."

"Still," he said, ambling over to join her, "if it got to Andrew before he comes off his drugs and back to his senses, that might set him back. Maybe it's better this way."

"It's difficult to know. Do you think I had better go see him once he's settled in?"

He held her gaze for a moment. "Tomorrow's Monday, and they probably won't allow visitors so soon after he arrived. Tuesday? We could go together."

It was on the tip of her tongue to say she was perfectly capable of driving a buggy seven miles. But something in his eyes made her hold her tongue.

"I would feel better if I were with you," he said.

"Why?" She couldn't imagine it was for the pleasure of her company.

"Just in case he remembers. And is ... angry."

"Angry that *der Herr* sent someone to save his life?"

"No. Angry that—" His throat seemed to close. "If he's gone back to his *Englisch* ways unbeknownst to us, he might not be happy about his situation. The church paying for everything. People thinking he's engaged to an Amish woman. All of it."

"Oh." Rebecca could sort of see that. It might be nice to have Noah's company if such were the case.

"I can see a *but* in your face," he said. "I didn't mean to scare you."

"It's just that …" She might as well tell him the truth, even if he rolled his eyes at her. "I just thought I might go on my own. In case I'm able to see him alone. Speak to him when he's in his right mind. That is, if he's not in the state you say. If he still thinks he's Amish."

"I can step out of the room." He looked puzzled.

She turned away, walking slowly, unseeingly, between the two rows of trees. "I wondered if there might be a chance to— to find out if there could be … something."

"Something where?" Now she'd really lost him, and no wonder.

"Between us," she got out at last. She waited, her back to him, expecting the sound of laughter.

But there was nothing but the rustle and tap of the breeze among the branches. A moment passed. Two. She bent to pick a stem of last year's grass, to give her hands something to do, and turned.

His eyes looked stricken, just for a moment, before he ducked his head and the brim of his hat concealed his face. He pushed his hands into the pockets of his coat and closed the few steps between them. When his gaze met hers, she could see he had recovered his self-control.

"Is that what you want?" he asked. "Still? Even though he may be planning to turn *Englisch* again? Even though that girl is still out there and he may have feelings for her?"

She hadn't even considered that. His words rippled through her like a catspaw of wind on the river. She shivered, and fastened up her coat.

"If he does, it would be *gut* to know for sure and certain, *nix?*" she said, trying to keep her tone light yet reasonable. Though how Andrew might still have feelings for such a callous woman was beyond her.

"And then what?" Noah asked. "He says he wants to live *Englisch*, you just go home and forget him?"

"I suppose." Considering practically every waking moment had been consumed with thoughts of Andrew for months, she was a little surprised to realize that she hadn't been thinking of him nearly as much all week.

"And if he wants to live Amish?" Noah demanded. "What then?"

"Well, that's why I wanted to talk to him. To find out if … it's possible for him to have feelings for me."

He stepped back, as though she had pushed him. "I'll tell you what my feelings are," he said, sounding choked, two spots of color burning under his cheekbones. "I love my brother. I do. But you would be completely wasted on him. He's had so many girlfriends—Amish, *Englisch*, who knows—and left them. No matter how they felt about him. Because all he can see is the road leading away from wherever he is. Not the possibility of a life right where he's standing."

Rebecca stared at him, shocked to her toes.

And then his words sank in. *Wasted on him. You would be completely wasted on him.*

"Those are terrible things to say about your own brother." She felt as though she could hardly draw breath. His *eyes…*

"Doesn't mean they're not true."

146

And before she could take a breath to reply, one arm went around her back to pull her toward him. The other hand cupped her cheek.

"You deserve everything good," he said hoarsely, and when she took a breath to say something—anything—he angled his head and kissed her.

She felt like a balloon, expanding to the point of explosion. The world had turned upside down and faded to nothing— leaving only Noah's soft lips, the way they moved on hers, the way they made her want to press up against him, seeking warmth. Him. *More.*

With a gasp for breath, she realized how tightly her arms were wound around him. She stepped away. Cool air flowed in—along with sanity.

"We can't," she said, her mouth hardly able to form words.

Another step away. Two. Then she turned and ran out of the orchard, out of the canyon, away from the warmth and strength of Noah's arms.

"I'm sorry," she heard him call out. "I shouldn't have—"

But by then she had flown.

Fool! Noah berated himself, resting his forehead on his fists against the gnarled trunk of an apple tree. How could he have been so *deerich?* Saying those things about Andrew and by them, proving he was no better that his brother. Neither of them deserved her, and now he'd gone and taken himself out of the running by frightening her away, probably for good, because he hadn't been able to control his jealousy.

That's right. Jealousy.

Noah looked himself in the eye and didn't like what he saw.

Jealousy of a wounded man who had come back from the brink of death, thanks to Rebecca. Instead of running Andrew down, he should have focused on his good qualities. His sense of humor. His ability to laugh at himself. His willingness to work. All the rest of it might have been true, but did he have to blurt it out to Rebecca, who had just admitted she had feelings for him? Nobody liked the bearer of bad news, and he had just proved that for himself.

He hiked back down to the ranch house on unwilling feet, and sure enough, Rebecca was nowhere to be seen as his family took their leave. By his mother's face, he knew that someone had let it slip about Andrew's engagement—or lack thereof. At Aendi Annie's little *Daadi Haus*, supper was as uncomfortable as a meal could possibly be. Plates went down on the table with a slap. Knives and soup spoons clanked more loudly than they ought.

Until finally his mother burst out, "When were you *Kinner* going to tell your father and me that Andrew isn't engaged to Rebecca Miller after all? That it was a mistake? A misunderstanding?"

Patricia and Clara looked at one another, and began to eat as if their lives depended on it.

"Noah?" his father said. "Simeon? Your mother asked you a question."

"I had nothing to do with it." Sim spooned hot, rich beef barley soup into his mouth.

"It was the doctor," Noah said, since he had no choice, with both parents staring at him, accusation in their eyes. Could this day get any worse? "He said that we weren't to argue with

Andrew. If he believed he was engaged to Rebecca, we should play along so that we didn't stress his brain until he was off the drugs."

"Play along?" Mamm put her spoon down.

"Play along with a *lie?"* his father said incredulously.

"What could we do? Rebecca told me about the mistake that first night. If the doctor hadn't said what he did, I would have told you. Meanwhile, the girls and Aendi Annie went to church and talked about it—"

"Don't you drag me into this," Annie said. "I never believed it for a minute. That girl can disappear in an empty room— she didn't behave like an engaged woman at all."

For some reason this made Noah cranky on top of being on the defensive. "Well, anyway, except for the bishop, now the church believes it. But more important than that, as soon as we can, we need to find out if Andrew still believes it."

"What then?" Aendi Annie asked. "Does the poor boy really think he's engaged?"

"He did when we left him this morning," Mamm said grimly, running her spoon through her soup but not really eating it. "So did we. Oh, this is a terrible mess. What were you all thinking?"

There being no answer to that, Noah had left the table and soothed his feelings with a long tramp across the muddy fields.

The following day, he spent every waking hour except for meals working on the farmhouse with Simeon, who had no complaints about the pace he set. They took the kitchen cabinets down to be refinished, insulated the walls, then screwed the drywall in place, ready for tape and texture like the other rooms.

The Siksika Valley Neurological Rehabilitation Center called Annie's old cell phone that evening to say that Andrew had been transported there on schedule that afternoon, and had settled into his new situation well enough that they had already begun therapy. Dat asked about visiting, and was told that visitors were welcome at any time, not just within certain hours.

"They say family visits can be worked in as part of the patient's therapy," Dat said, making Mamm's face light up. "We'll go tomorrow morning."

"I'll go in the afternoon," Noah said. "Rebecca wanted to go, too."

The light drained out of his mother's face. "Why should she? What business does she have there now?"

"Andrew may have business with her," Dat reminded her gently. "What is she going to say to him?" he asked Noah.

"I think that depends on his state of mind," he said diplomatically. "Be careful what you say," he begged them.

"I'm certainly not going to let him believe a lie," Mamm snapped.

"But if he's still on the drugs and his mind isn't healed—"

"Don't worry. I'll talk to his doctor first." She glared at him. "That is, provided *he* hasn't been told to tell lies."

Noah had no choice but to hand the entire situation over to God. It was just too complicated and now that his parents knew the truth, out of anybody's control.

That night, beside Annie's sofa, where he was sleeping temporarily, he bowed his head over clasped hands.

Lieber Gott, please lend Your strength to my brother and help his mind to heal. Be with my parents, and help them see that we were doing what we thought was right at the time. Help them to forgive

Rebecca, who feels badly enough about this whole situation. I pray that Your goodness and mercy will see us all through, and that most of all, Andrew will realize that Your mighty hand has saved him for a higher purpose than merely taking his own way. Help me to help him, Father. Use me according to Your will. I pray these things in the name of Your holy Son.

He began to rise from his knees, then dropped back down.

Be with Rebecca, Father. Give her balm for her spirit—show her Your love. And help her to forgive me for yesterday in the orchard.

Even though he didn't regret that kiss.

Not one bit. Not when it thrilled his soul just to remember it.

CHAPTER 15

Tuesday after lunch, Rebecca was backing Hester between the rails of the buggy when Noah walked through the open doors into the barn. With a nod of greeting, he silently began to fasten the buckles, and Hester was harnessed and ready to go in just a few minutes.

"Denki," she said. "Would you like to drive?"

Another nod, and she climbed in on his left. "I would have picked you up," she said. "It's quite a walk over here from Annie's." Every bit of three miles. Had he even had any lunch?

"I needed it." He clucked to Hester, and for a moment, the only sound was the rattle of the buggy and Hester's hooves on the gravel of the lane. "Walking helps me think."

Was he thinking about Sunday? she wondered. About that kiss? But she was too embarrassed to ask. "Silence helps me," she offered instead.

He glanced at her. "Does that mean you want me to be quiet?"

With a smile, she shook her head. *"Neh.* But sometimes,

when I need to make a decision, or think something over, I go someplace quiet. Like the orchard."

Oh, why had she said that? If only she could call her words back.

"Rebecca, I'm sorry," he said, as quickly as if he'd been waiting for the opening. "What happened— That was forward of me, and disrespectful to you. I hope you'll forgive me. It was a mistake."

Kissing her was a mistake?

She shrank deeper into her coat, thankful for her black away bonnet. In its depths, her face was concealed from his view completely.

"I forgive you," she croaked.

They turned onto the highway, and Hester picked up speed. The silence seemed to stretch away to the horizon and instead of simply accepting it, like she would any other day, something drove her to speak.

"I don't plan to tell Andrew about the orchard, if that worries you."

He coughed, as though air had caught in his throat. "It doesn't. I hadn't thought of any such thing." With a sigh, he went on, "I suppose it's just one more secret to keep."

She didn't want to be anybody's secret. Or their mistake.

"All the secrets may be out in the open after today," she said.

"Except that one."

Fine. She would keep his *mistake* a secret. So well that for the next seven miles, she rode silently beside him. He didn't seem inclined to talk any more, either.

Whatever, as the *Englisch* girls said.

At the clinic, they found to their surprise that there was a horse shed, with a shiny rail where she could tie Hester's rein. Clearly someone had told the builders their project was in the middle of Amish country. Rebecca could only be grateful that they didn't have to unhitch Hester and lead her over to one of the newly planted saplings. She'd probably graze on its buds and then they'd be in trouble.

After inquiring at reception, they were directed down a gleaming hallway, not nearly as cluttered with carts and medications and equipment as the county hospital had been. The rooms were painted light, soothing colors like pale yellow, cream, and the blue of a high summer sky. They found Andrew being settled into his bed by a nurse.

"Noah!" he said, pushing himself up on the pillows as the nurse departed. "Nice timing. I just got back from therapy."

"How are you doing?" Noah crossed the room to take a chair by the bed.

Rebecca was just as happy to stand by the window, which had its own sapling right outside. Some day it would be a pretty tree of some kind, maybe a poplar.

"You'd have to ask the therapist, but I think I'm doing all right," Andrew said. "You know, *Bruder*, much as I like you, I'd rather look at Rebecca there in the chair."

Noah and Rebecca both froze. Then Noah seemed to recover and offered the chair to Rebecca with a movement of one hand.

There was no getting out of it.

She rounded the foot of the bed and they traded places. "I'm glad you're feeling all right," she offered shyly. Even in a hospital bed and green pajamas, Andrew's smile still took her breath away.

"They tell me that the neurons in my brain—little bits of

electricity, I guess—need to re-learn how to connect so that my leg moves naturally. Right now I have to sort of force it into motion. It's not automatic. But a little at a time, I think I'll get it."

"That's *gut*," she said. "How is the fracture? And the shoulder?"

"Both doing well, I think. The shoulder isn't as sore as it was at first." He moved it gingerly in its sling. "They say I can have this off any day now, but complete healing will take a couple of months."

"How long do you have to stay here?" Noah asked.

Andrew shrugged the uninjured shoulder. "Until my neuro therapist says I'm well enough to go, I guess. Believe me, if it wasn't for that, I'd be out of here today. I can live with a fractured tibia and a dislocated shoulder, but the rest of it makes it hard."

"The church will pay for it," Rebecca assured him. "My father spoke with one of the board members and got a discount."

"So Mamm and Dat told me." He grinned. "It was kind of your father to do that."

"Kind of Brock Madison, you mean. He owns the Double Diamond, the dude ranch down the road from us. They're very well off, but they get on well enough with our people. We have to stick together, we ranch folks. You never know when something bad will happen and you need your neighbors."

She fell silent. Since when had she become such a nervous *Plappermaul?*

"Like me, needing you," he said, his gaze warm on her. "They told me what you did."

Heat burned in her cheeks, and she ducked her head. *"Der*

Herr led me there to the right place and time. Do you remember what happened?"

He shook his head. "I remember leaving Amity on the bus. I think I remember seeing the Rockies, but I don't know whether it was from the east or west. And then I woke up in the hospital."

"So the whole month is a blank?"

Again that one-shoulder shrug.

"What about working on Aendi Annie's house?" Noah asked. "Do you remember anything about that?"

Andrew's face seemed to settle, or flatten, as though he didn't want to answer him. "Was I supposed to work on a house?"

"You were," he said, "All the supplies were ordered in advance."

"We had a work party on Friday and got nearly everything done that you would have in a month," Rebecca assured him. "With the supplies there, all the men had to do was get started."

Andrew gazed at Noah. "So I was supposed to come out here and work on Mamm and Dat's new place?" When Noah nodded, he said, "Huh," as though this was all news to him.

Hadn't their parents mentioned it during their visit this morning?

"How is your brain?" Rebecca found the courage to ask. There had been no mention of bears or kittens yet. That had to be a *gut* sign. "Are you still seeing things?"

"How would I know?" He laughed, and the sound made Rebecca smile. "What I mean is—I remember the doctors walking the bears on leashes just as clearly as I remember Mamm at my bedside, or you."

"You remember her at your bedside?" Noah asked sharply. Then he amended in a softer tone, "We weren't sure how much you were aware of, those first days."

"I was aware of her." His gaze found Rebecca's. "You were there, *nix*? You weren't a hallucination?"

Oh, how she wished she could say yes, that she and every silly word she'd said had been due to the drugs.

"I was there," she said softly.

He reached over and took her hand. "I knew it. I couldn't make up someone as pretty as you. You even sang to me, didn't you?"

He was holding her hand. Another dream come true.

Except his fingers were so smooth they felt almost like those of a doll. As though he'd never done a day's work in his life. Smooth, and too warm. Did hands get like this in the hospital? Was there something in the soap?

"I did," she said, sliding her fingers from his gentle grip. "One of the ones Cora Swarey sings, do you remember? In Amity? 'Walk a Little While,' it's called."

He hummed the first notes of the chorus.

"It's amazing you can remember something as small as that, but the whole past month is a blank," Noah said, shaking his head. "Do the doctors think your memory will come back?"

Andrew nodded. *"Ja*, but *when* is another question. But yet, I remembered about the house we're going to build. Isn't that something?"

Rebecca closed her eyes. *Give me strength, dear Lord.* When she opened them, both brothers were gazing at her. One in expectation, and one in ... warning?

"*Ja*, it's something," she said weakly. "But I was just telling a story."

"It didn't sound like a story," he said. "It sounded real. Like we had made plans."

Noah pushed himself off the window frame. "Guess I'll try to find the restroom."

She had wanted time alone with Andrew, and now she had it. Somehow having one's dreams come true didn't feel quite the way she'd expected. It felt like ... walking a path where you knew a trap had been set. You just couldn't quite see where it was. There were too many zigzags in the trail.

"Rebecca?" Andrew said. "It wasn't a story, was it? We really are making plans."

She dared to lift her gaze to his. "You sound as though you think that might be *gut*."

"I do think that." He took her hand again. "They told me we were engaged. I should have remembered proposing, but I don't. Is it true?"

The trail straightened out and suddenly she saw there was no trap. Not if she told him what was true, once and for all. *Now is the time,* a still, small voice whispered in her mind. *Tell him.*

"Those things really were just a story," she said, straightening in the chair. "We're not engaged. The staff at the hospital misunderstood, when I came in the ambulance with you that night."

He stared at her.

She went on, "But it turned out to be all right, because they let me into the ICU and let me stay with you. They said that people under sedation might still be able to hear what's going on around them. I told you stories and sang to you so you'd know you weren't alone."

"Why do my parents think you're my fiancée, then?" His eyebrows drew into a frown. "They said you were. They were happy about it."

She rolled her shoulders uncomfortably, and wished there was a graceful way to pull her hand from his a second time. "The misunderstanding. The staff at the county hospital told them, because that's what they thought. It's all right now, though. Your parents know we're not."

"They didn't say a word about it this morning. Not even when I asked if you were coming."

"They probably wanted me to tell you," was all she could manage to say. What must Kate and Arlon think of her now? "You're not to worry about it," she added. "You're to get well, *nix?*"

"I don't have much choice about that," he said, his humor returning. "They're pretty firm around here. They expect me to work at getting well like it's my job."

"I suppose in a way it is. Without doing that, you won't be able to do your real job, will you?"

"One follows the other," he agreed. After a little silence, he said, "So you've met all my family?"

"*Ja.* Though I've known your Aendi Annie my whole life. I think most of the *Youngie* in the district can say that. She's the oldest member of our church."

"So she gets a chair up front on Sundays. Have I met her?"

She was finally able to look him in the eye, now that the topic was safe. "I'm sure you must have, as a child. Maybe when your memory comes back, you'll remember her."

"It seems funny." He frowned and finally released her

159

hand. "That I was supposed to come here, but I don't remember a thing about it. Are you sure I didn't?"

"We would have noticed," she told him with a smile.

If he was Amish. But if he was running with an *Englisch* crowd, and that woman at the wheel of that car, would Rebecca have seen him as she ran errands in the valley? Wasn't one of the signs of love being able to sense the beloved even when you couldn't see them? Maybe that was just a story, too.

Her illusions about true love were dropping one by one, like leaves in autumn. At this rate, her little tree of belief would be quite bare.

"Then where was I, if I wasn't in Amity and I wasn't here?"

She couldn't answer that. "When *Gott* restores your memory, everything will become clear," she told him. "Maybe you shouldn't try to push it. Funny things bring memory to mind, don't they? The way the smell of roses always makes me think of the one trip our whole family made to New Mexico to visit my aunt. My sister and I weren't even in school yet, but I remember Aendi had roses hanging over the front door of her adobe house in a big, luxurious arch. The scent of them was *wunderbaar*."

He was still frowning, absently rubbing the underside of the sling, and she subsided. Probably he didn't want to hear about silly things like roses, when he had more important concerns.

There were steps outside the door and she turned, expecting Noah. But it was a man in scrubs with a badge on a lanyard that said McMichael, MD.

"Hey, Andrew," he greeted him. He glanced at Rebecca, who got up and moved out of the way.

"Doctor, this is ... well, I thought she was my fiancée, but I guess she isn't." He frowned as though he still couldn't quite believe it.

"What, did she just break up with you?" The doctor checked a series of numbers on a tablet. "If so, you seem in pretty good spirits."

"No, she didn't. It's a weird situation."

"If you say so," the doctor said. "Your therapist says she thinks you can manage a stroll outside. What do you think?"

"I'm in," Andrew said at once. "Can Rebecca come?"

"If she wants."

Where was Noah? How long did a visit to the restroom take? "It's getting late," she said hastily, "and we have seven miles to go in the buggy. I'll come again another day, all right?"

He had already swung his legs to the side of the bed, and the doctor rolled the walker up to him so he could put his weight on it.

"Promise?" Andrew asked, testing his balance without looking at her.

"I promise."

Neither of them noticed when she slipped out of the room. Which was fine. His job was to get well and do what the doctor said, not stand around talking with someone he hadn't even spoken to before that awful night.

Noah met her at the junction where the corridor gave onto the bright, sunny lobby and the reception desk. "Where have you been?"

The doors swooshed open and they went outside. At the side of the parking lot, Hester lifted her head, as though she'd been waiting for the sight of them.

"I thought I'd give you some time together," Noah said, buttoning his coat.

"What for?" She buttoned hers, then patted Hester's nose before she untied the hitching rein. He took the driving reins and she backed Hester out of the three-sided shed, then went around to climb in on the passenger side.

He shook the reins over the horse's back and the buggy lurched into motion. "Why else would you drive seven miles to see him?"

"You drove," she pointed out. Then she turned to stare at him, the same stare Mamm often used when she wanted the truth, and no beating around the bush. "What's going on, Noah? First you don't want me to be engaged to him. Now you want us to spend time together. Have you changed your mind, or are you just trying to make me all *verhuddelt?*"

"I'm *verhuddelt* enough for both of us," he mumbled. At the end of the long, curving drive he turned onto the highway and let Hester settle into a comfortable pace. Then, louder, he said, "I thought that was what you wanted."

She snorted. "That was literally the first time I've spoken to him. When he was conscious," she amended. "I didn't say a thing that you couldn't have heard. Including when I told him we weren't engaged, and all those silly things I said while he was sleeping were just a story."

He was so surprised that the reins went limp in his hands, and Hester looked over her shoulder to see what was the matter. Noah recovered himself and took control once again.

"You told him. Point blank."

"I'm sick to death of the damage I've done by not speaking up. By waffling when I should have just told the truth. So I did. As you say, point blank."

"How did he take it?"

His hands were still a little tight on the reins. "Do you want me to drive?"

"Neh. How did he take it?"

With a shrug, she said, "Well, considering he's only thought he was engaged for something like three days, it wasn't as though I broke his heart, if that's what you're thinking."

"I don't know what I'm thinking." He huffed a laugh and shook his head. "I'm just amazed that you told him. Considering all those things you said in the ICU. About building a house and all that."

Did he have to bring that up?

"I thought you really did have feelings for him."

"So did I," she confessed. "But…"

"But?"

"His hands are so smooth."

He gaped at her, but controlled the reins before Hester could react. "Now you're not making any sense."

"I'm making perfect sense. Noah, when did he leave Amity? The date, I mean."

After a moment's thought, he said, "Right around the first week of March."

"And how long does it take for a man's hands to recover from being a carpenter?"

"I have no idea. I've been a carpenter pretty much continuously since I was fourteen. So has Sim. But there wasn't much work for us in the New Year. Just little indoor jobs. What are you getting at?"

"Andrew has definitely not been doing carpentry work lately, here or anywhere else. Even if he was living *Englisch* while he was here in the valley, he would have had to support himself. And if it wasn't doing carpentry, what was he doing?"

"You'll have to ask him."

"I did. It's all a blank."

"What does it matter? The one thing we do know is that he wasn't here when we thought he was, and the work didn't get done."

"*Ja,* exactly. I think he was off joyriding with that woman. In the car. The one who left him for dead that night."

He eyed her, then returned his attention to the road when a mud-spattered pickup pulled out to pass them with a roar of its engine. "I still don't know what you're getting at," he said when they could hear each other speak once more.

"My feelings for him were … a dream." She forced the words out. "I wove a dream there in the ICU, and it's my own fault that he heard me and remembers it. But how can he remember that and not where he was for a month?"

"The brain is a mysterious thing," Noah said. "Like the heart, only *Gott* knows it."

"What I'm getting at is, how can I have feelings for a man I don't know, and whose behavior is strange, to say the least? I had a little crush, and made a fool of myself, but that's all over now."

He was silent, waiting for her to go on.

She made up her mind. "If anyone asks me, I'll tell them we've broken it off. It's over. Done."

"Except that isn't the exact truth, either, is it?" He kept his gaze on the road, between Hester's ears. "There was never anything to break off."

"All right, then, I'll just say that it was a misunderstanding that got blown out of proportion. Is that better?"

"It's the truth. Nothing better than that."

Well, at least they agreed on something. For the next five miles, she made sure they talked about anything but Andrew. She told him about who was ranching what land as they passed fences and property lines on both sides of the highway. He had met many of the men during the work party, but you couldn't separate a family from their land around here. They went together.

He asked good questions, cementing each person in his mind. Which was funny, considering he didn't plan to stay more than a few weeks.

It wasn't until she dropped him off at the lane leading up to the King farmhouse and was continuing on her way that she realized something had been simmering just under the surface of her mind.

"It's strange, Hester," she said to the horse. Hester's ear flicked toward her, as though she was listening. "He said I was pretty. He held my hand. He smiled that beautiful smile I've been dreaming about because that was all I had. But you know what?"

Hester didn't.

"He never asked me a single thing about myself. Not one question about my family, or what they thought of this whole situation, or anything. What do you suppose that means?"

The horse trotted on, as though the answer were unknowable.

"Do you think I'm being selfish? Wanting someone to think about me first?"

No one had ever accused her of that. Because she'd never given anyone a reason to.

"Our whole conversation was about him, Hester. That

doesn't seem right, does it?" she said. "Courtship is supposed to be an equal give and take. The way Mamm and Dat are. Interested in each other, and what the other is doing, even though our days are pretty similar, and they've had umpteen gazillion days together already."

Hester nodded with each brisk step.

"At least Noah asks me things as though he cares about my answer," she said. "I may not *want* to answer, and sometimes he makes me irritated and annoyed, but at least he asks. He's honest about things. And don't go thinking I have any interest in Noah King at all."

Hester snorted.

Rebecca raised her eyebrows at her horse, then saw that they were passing the Circle M pastures. In the distance, Adam and Zach recognized the buggy and raised their hands in greeting, then wheeled the horses around to begin checking another section of fence.

Hester had just caught sight of the other animals, that was all.

CHAPTER 16

aomi Miller's body clock was all backward and upside down. She was in a perpetual state of sleep deprivation, and she and little Deborah often napped together between feedings. Day or night, she was so tired that that all she could think of was the next time the baby fell asleep so that she could do the same.

It was sometime after midnight, and the fire popped softly in the woodstove, its comforting heat reaching Naomi and Deborah in the upholstered rocker that had become theirs, not hers alone. Reuben was asleep in their bedroom, so she had brought Deborah out here for her feeding so as not to disturb him.

When a light step sounded on the stairs, Naomi recognized it as female. It couldn't be Malena, who slept like the dead, so it had to be either Sara or Rebecca.

"*Dochder?*" she said quietly.

In the kitchen, the faucet ran in two spurts, and Rebecca came into the living room with a glass of water in each hand.

"*Denki, Liebschdi,*" Naomi said, and drank deeply. She set

the glass on the little end table Reuben had made for their fifth anniversary, the "wood" one. He hadn't intended to, *Englisch* ceremonies not being top of his mind, but it had been a nice coincidence. "What are you doing up and about?"

"I can't sleep. Has she finished nursing?" When Naomi nodded, Rebecca put her own glass of water on the coffee table and bent to take Deborah into her arms. She sat in her corner of the sofa, laid the towel over her shoulder, and patted the *Boppli*'s back in a slow rhythm.

"Is something on your mind?" Naomi corrected herself. "Besides this situation with Andrew King?"

"There isn't a situation now," she said. "I told you all at dinner, remember?"

"Oh, I remember. But there are things that a woman just can't say in front of her grown brothers, ain't so?"

Rebecca smiled. "How well you know me, Mamm."

"Do I, dear one? Until tonight I never would have believed you could talk so frankly to any man other than your father. Never mind a man we hardly knew existed until last Friday. It seems so unlike you to be in this situation at all."

"I know." Deborah burped and Rebecca wiped her little rosebud mouth with a corner of the towel. "But now Andrew knows it was all a mistake, and his parents and family know. The bishop knows." Her voice faltered.

"What is it?" Naomi asked gently.

"It's Tuesday already—"

"Wednesday," Naomi said with a glance at her engagement clock on the oak mantel. "As of an hour ago."

"Even worse. I still don't know if I'm to be baptized on Sunday, Mamm. I'm worried that the bishop won't let me go up with Sara and Josh and Malena."

"I'm sure he will." Naomi couldn't see a reason why he wouldn't, but the pleat between her daughter's brows must be smoothed away somehow. "You've had the courage to speak the truth to everyone concerned. And soon enough, the rest of the church will know that it was all a misunderstanding. I'm sure most of them do already. Sadie and Ruby wouldn't have let it go without correcting whoever they were talking to. I know we haven't."

Rebecca's chest lifted and fell in a sigh. "I hope you're right."

"If it's weighing on you, then go back over to Wengerds' tomorrow. In the morning. If all goes well with Daniel and Lovina and they arrive in the afternoon with the moving van, then it will be too crazy around here to get away. Best to go while it's quiet."

And there was the smoothing out of her dear girl's forehead as she smiled. "I can't wait to see them. And little Joel. Daniel will be so happy to meet his tiny *Schweschder*." She looked down at the baby on her shoulder. "She's asleep."

"I'll take her, and you can put another piece of wood in the stove."

Rebecca put the baby in Naomi's arms, and tended to the fire. But still she didn't say *guder nacht*. "Mamm?"

"*Ja?*"

"How do you know when someone cares about you? I mean, *really* cares. The kind that lasts, like you and Dat."

This was *not* what Naomi had been expecting. She must choose her words carefully, so as not to frighten Rebecca away like a sparrow. "Sometimes it's difficult at first, when a person is coming to grips with their feelings," she said. "Why?

Did Andrew say something to make you think he cares, after all?"

The little frown was back between her girl's winglike brows, but it was more thoughtful than worried. "I told Noah that Andrew has only known about me for three days, so it wasn't like I broke his heart with the news that it was all a mistake."

Noah. Naomi's maternal antennae began to quiver.

"Andrew and I talked after I got the truth off my chest, but mostly it was all about him."

Naomi allowed herself a smile. "From what I understood, he's been your favorite subject for some time."

She couldn't tell whether Rebecca blushed, or if it was just the firelight in the darkened room. "I know. But if he cared about me, even a little, wouldn't he want to know things about me? Ask about my family and such?"

"That's the usual way of getting to know someone," Naomi conceded.

"I mean, he did think we were engaged for three days."

"Maybe he thought you'd already had those getting-to-know-you conversations before you were engaged, and his memory just wasn't cooperating."

"But how could he think that when we've never spoken? I told Noah that today was the first actual conversation I'd ever had with his brother." She frowned at the stove, then got up to close down the damper.

Noah again. Naomi's antennae had not been mistaken.

"Sounds like you and Noah have been talking things over."

She shrugged. "I suppose. We didn't have much to say on the way in, though, once I—"

Naomi waited a beat, but Rebecca simply stood in front of

the stove with her arms wrapped around her waist, as though she were cold.

Or protecting herself.

"Once you?" Naomi prompted gently.

Another beat. "Once I brought up the orchard."

"And what about the orchard would silence the two of you?" The minute the words were out of her mouth, Naomi knew. *"Liebschdi,* did something happen when Noah went up to get you the other day?"

With a sigh that seemed to come from the bottom of her heart, Rebecca sank to the rug and laid her head on Naomi's knee. "He kissed me."

She tried not to react, but Rebecca must have felt the quiver that went through her, and lifted her head.

And she'd said nothing about it? Even to her sister? No, she couldn't have. Malena couldn't keep a secret if her life depended on it.

"You've been kissed by boys before, haven't you?" Naomi said softly, carefully, touching Rebecca's hair, loosely braided for the night. "Was there something about this one?"

Rebecca leaned her forehead on Naomi's knee once more. *"Ja.* It was *wunderbaar.* Like I was falling up into the sky."

Oh, my. "I know that feeling." Her voice was warm with the happiness in her own memories. She couldn't help it. Even now, Reuben's kiss could make her knees go weak. "Is that why you wanted to know how a woman knows when a man really cares?"

The shining blond head moved up and down.

"Did any of the boys you kissed before make you feel this way?"

Back and forth. *Neh.*

"Then it seems you might get to know Noah better."

Rebecca lifted her head and their gazes met. "But he's leaving. The fifteenth of May at the latest. They're all going back to Amity."

"There are such things as letters," Naomi said mildly.

"I know, but … I don't think his heart is in it. I think he wants to stay for spring turnout. To try cowboying instead of carpentering."

"He's a grown man," Naomi said. "He could do that if he really wanted to."

"But that would mean disappointing Simeon. They're in business together. It would be hard on him."

"Ah," Naomi said. She wasn't certain which of the brothers she meant. Both, perhaps. "And yet, he kissed you."

"And yet, he kissed me," Rebecca echoed. "Even knowing that he was leaving. So how can he care? Why would he do that?"

Naomi figured it wouldn't be very fair to say, *Because you are as pretty as a spring blossom, and there you were in a magical place, and sometimes a person can be confused yet still be overcome by their emotions.*

No, she couldn't say that. "If it happens again, you might ask him," she said instead, still in that gentle tone she might use to an easily frightened creature. "Because you are a Miller, and you don't deserve to be toyed with, if that's what he's doing."

"It didn't feel like that was what he was doing." Her daughter sat close enough that now Naomi could see the blush in her cheeks. "It felt like he meant it."

Perhaps his kiss confessed what his words could not.

But Naomi couldn't very well say that, either.

"If he's leaving, he must be honest with you. If the two of you have feelings for each other, you may have to deal with real life. And consequences greater than simply gossip in the church. If such feelings were to come between him and his brother …" Naomi thought of Simeon, so responsible, so grim. Like Daniel might have been if Lovina hadn't come back into his life and saved him from himself.

"I don't want that," Rebecca said quietly. "But it may all come to nothing." She got to her feet with an air of bringing their conversation to a close, and leaned over to kiss the baby's rounded cheek. "The most important thing is Sunday, and after that, Daniel's wedding. Are you going to put Deborah down and try to get some sleep?"

"*Ja.*" Naomi struggled up out of her chair. Her stomach muscles would be back to their normal usefulness at some point, but that point had not arrived yet.

Rebecca's arms slid around her waist in a soft hug. "*Denki,* Mamm. For being you. And for being my mother."

Tears prickled in Naomi's eyes. With her arms full of sleeping infant, she could only tilt her head and kiss Rebecca's forehead. "And you, for being such a loving and sensible young woman. *Der Herr* has a plan for you, *Liebschdi.* We just need to wait for Him to reveal it."

Rebecca nodded. And then she twinkled into a smile. "And in the meantime, stay out of orchards." Lightly, so as not to disturb her sleeping family, Rebecca ran up the stairs to her room.

"Easier said than done, I think," Naomi whispered, smiling, and carried Deborah off to bed.

CHAPTER 17

*R*uby Wengerd walked Rebecca out to the springhouse, where her father was clearing a blocked filter.

"I'm certain there will be nothing to prevent you from being baptized," she said, linking Rebecca's arm in hers the way they had done as little scholars, walking to the one-room schoolhouse together. The bishop had donated that triangle of land and a sturdy log building had been built by the same outfit that had built the ranch house at the Circle M. "Now that it's known that the engagement was just a misunderstanding. And from what you tell me, you've done all you can to make it right."

"I hope he agrees with you." Rebecca squeezed her friend's arm and then approached the springhouse alone. She leaned in the door of the little log building, which smelled of cool water and cedar shelving where the bishop's mother had once cooled her milk and made butter. *"Guder mariye,* Bishop."

He set his pliers aside and wiped his wet hands on his

pants. "Hallo, Rebecca. I seem to remember I owe you an answer about something important, don't I?"

"Only if the *gut Gott* has given it to you," she said. "I don't want to presume."

Water from the spring ran under the springhouse to form a creek that eventually joined the Siksika River. Little Joe walked along its shallow bank, where a trail indicated this was a favorite walk, and she went with him. The pussy willows were mature now, and had become yellow tassels. There were even a couple of crocuses pushing their purple and yellow heads out into the sunshine. When they reached the split rail fence that divided the yard from the first of his cattle paddocks, he leaned his forearms on the top rail.

Dat did the same, Rebecca reflected. He'd often stand like this, gazing out over the land with a kind of quiet happiness at being chosen by the Lord to be its steward.

"The *gut Gott* didn't take long to set my mind at ease," Little Joe said. "I hear you've been to see the young man in hospital."

"Yesterday," Rebecca replied. "I told him the truth. That I had said something silly—more than a few somethings—and the staff misunderstood. That we weren't engaged after all."

"How did he take it?" The bishop glanced at her.

"He seemed more puzzled than unhappy," she admitted. "But then, before yesterday I hadn't really spoken to him. While he was awake, that is. So I didn't exactly break his heart."

"You might have broken his mother's," he said.

Rebecca looked up in alarm. "What do you mean?"

"From what I understand, Andrew King has left the church before, more than once, intending to live *Englisch*."

"I know. Noah told me."

"This is his third attempt to walk the narrow way. His parents were pretty happy that their prayers had been answered and he'd found a girl who would walk by his side. Help him. Settle him down."

"I think Andrew would do better if he'd let God settle him down. Not an ordinary woman."

Little Joe turned from the view to gaze at her. "Can't argue with you there. It's a big expectation to put on someone." When she only nodded, he went on, "But that isn't your path to walk, and I have to say I'm glad about that. Your path is the path of acceptance, and obedience to our Father's will. So I'll be calling your name on Sunday, along with your brother and sister and Sara Fischer, and welcoming you into fellowship."

Ever since he'd said God had set his mind at ease, Rebecca had known there would be nothing preventing her baptism. Still, hearing the words spoken aloud brought tears to her eyes. *"Denki,* Bishop."

He nodded, pretending not to see her emotion, and turned to go back to his work in the springhouse. "Shame those boys are set on returning to Colorado," he said, apropos of nothing. "Josiah and John Bontrager have helped most of us build our homes and barns, but they're getting on now. It would be nice to have younger men coming up in the church with that kind of ability."

Josiah and John Bontrager were related somehow to Susan's father. They'd been born bachelors. Susan said they would probably die bachelors, too, because no woman in the valley with any sense would marry one knowing she'd be cooking and cleaning for both. Mamm tended to disagree. Anyway, they were in their sixties now, and it was certainly true that some new blood would be good for the community.

Not that she was thinking of Noah and Simeon's blood specifically, mind you.

She left the bishop to his work with steps much lighter than when she'd arrived, and waved at Ruby through the window as she passed the house. The only thing that disturbed her sunny mood was the knowledge that she'd unwittingly dealt Kate King such a blow, after giving her such joy. It was difficult not to feel responsible, as silly as she'd been to allow the whole thing to blow up out of control. So she could only pray that Kate and Arlon would find peace with the situation as it was now.

And that Andrew would find peace as well, and come to love the Amish life as his family did.

"THEY'RE HERE!" Malena shrieked at a quarter to two that afternoon. She'd been fluttering back and forth between the living room window, which gave just a glimpse of the highway between trees and fields, and the kitchen, where she was supposed to be putting trays of cookies in the oven. "In a big white box van with a buggy on a trailer!"

There was a stampede for coats and hats, as the family streamed down the stairs to meet the van as it trundled up the gravel lane. Whirling at the last minute, Rebecca pulled the last sheet of peanut butter cookies out of the oven and turned it off. That would be a fine greeting for her brother and his bride-to-be—a cloud of black smoke and the smell of burned peanut butter.

The van came to a halt and all its doors burst open.

"Mammi! Daed!" Nine-year-old Joel flung himself into his soon-to-be grandfather's arms. When his toes touched the ground once more, he did the same to his future grandmother and all his future aunts and uncles, and even slowed down enough to give little Nathan a smacking kiss. "Where's the other *Boppli?*" he asked, his brown eyes shining at the thought of cousins living so close, even though they wouldn't be big enough to play with for a few years yet.

"In her crib, asleep," Sara said with a laugh. "You'll meet her when she wakes up."

Adam and Zach gave their brother and future sister-in-law hugs of greeting, and then took Joel off to the barn with them to reacquaint him with all the horses he had said he missed in his letters.

Rebecca hugged her brother, too, and kissed Lovina, who was so lovely in her happiness that it almost took her breath away.

"Being engaged to my brother seems to suit you," she told her with a smile. Everyone knew that true beauty came from within, the result of an obedient spirit that pleased the Lord, but Rebecca knew that love had a lot to do with it, too.

"It does," Lovina confessed so readily that Mamm laughed. "I never imagined that I could be so happy."

"And I never imagined that Daniel could be," Malena said with her usual thoughtless honesty. "He looks like a different man, and it's not because he's had a haircut."

"Poor Daniel, saddled with a bride who can't cut hair to save her life," Lovina said. "I have to make it up to him in good cooking, I guess." She grinned, her grey eyes sparkling, as though Daniel had made it plain which he preferred.

"Dat, the driver has to get the van down to Libby to the rental place by five o'clock, or we pay for another day," Daniel said. "I'd like to take him down to the house to unload."

"We surely can," Reuben said. "Who's coming?"

"Me!" Joel shouted, running out of the barn. "And Zach and Adam and Josh, too. Zach says we can buy two buggy horses at the auction next month, Mamm. Can I name them?"

"Can I stop you?" Lovina said with a laugh. "Come away from the trailer. The men need to get the buggy off and put it in this barn until the horses come."

Zach released Lovina's buggy from its moorings on the trailer and the four brothers rolled it down a pair of metal ramps the driver had pulled out of the van. When the buggy landed on the ground with a bounce, Joel cheered.

"All right," Lovina called to her son once the buggy had been rolled into the barn next to the Miller vehicles. "Back in the van. We have a lot to do in an hour."

But many hands made light work, and by four o'clock, the van was unloaded, all its contents disgorged into the waiting rooms of Daniel's house, and the driver trundled away with a cheery wave.

"Of course Daniel would marry a woman who marks each box with the room it's supposed to go into," Malena confided to Rebecca as they carted boxes into the bedroom wing. "Daniel and Lovina's bedroom. Noah's bedroom. Living room. Kitchen cookware. Kitchen dishes. Do their brains hurt at the end of the day? Or does it come naturally?"

"I like an organized person, myself," Rebecca told her. Much as she loved Malena, *organized* was not the first word you'd use to describe her. "The alternative is that you pile everything in the middle of the living room and have to open every single box to find your frying pan."

"How is it we can be twins?" Malena groaned and went to get another armload.

When the boxes were all distributed into the rooms designated for them, Joshua asked Lovina if she wanted them to unpack everything as well.

"Oh, no indeed," she said. "I have been so looking forward to putting my home together. I want that job all to myself."

"Careful what you say." Daniel dropped a kiss on her heart-shaped Whinburg Township *Kapp* as he passed her with a big box labeled Quilts. "It took us days to pack it all up. It will take that long to put it all away."

"But what fun we'll have," she said with a laugh. "Daniel and Joel will sleep over here until the wedding," she confided to Rebecca and Malena. "I bet I'll find more done each morning when I come over than I left the night before. You just watch. They're both just as excited as I am about making a home together."

When the sun lowered behind the pines, they all walked back to the ranch house in a straggling bunch, talking and exchanging news with every step. In the kitchen, they found Mamm and Sara giving an elk roast its final basting. There were potatoes baked in their skins, creamed corn, and golden orange butternut squash mashed with butter and brown sugar. Out came the carrot and bean pickles they'd put up last autumn, and Malena's favorite, reddish-purple beet pickles flavored ever so faintly with clove.

Though they usually gave silent thanks for a meal, tonight Dat raised his voice in prayer.

"Dear Lord, thank You for bringing our children back to

us again, and for the blessing of their impending marriage. Thank You for the four who will be committing their lives to You on Sunday, and for the church, which will support them in love as they take their first steps. Thank You for this food, for the loving hands that prepared it, and most of all, for the sacrifice of Your Son that made all these gifts possible. We ask in Christ's holy name."

"Amen," Rebecca's family chorused quietly.

As cutlery began to clatter in serving bowls and Dat carved the savory, fragrant roast, Rebecca looked around the big farm table. Every seat was filled, plus a couple of extra. Everyone she loved was here, talking a mile a minute and filling their plates with food that they had grown or hunted or traded for with their neighbors. Only the squash and the coffee had come from the grocery store in Mountain Home.

Surely God was *gut* to them. And with the wedding on the twenty-ninth, that blessing would be increased as Daniel left the home in which he'd grown up, and walked with his wife and adopted son down the gravel lane to their own house.

"I've got a few days yet to finish the last details," he said in answer to Dat's question. "Like screwing the porcelain knobs Lovina picked out on the cupboard doors. Hanging a Coleman lamp over the kitchen table."

"And another coat of varnish on the bedroom doors," she said. "You told me you wanted them to glow like silk."

"I did," he said, smiling into her eyes. "It delights me to think of the workmanship of those little details, because they'll make the house more comfortable and beautiful for you."

"No coming in with muddy boots, then," she murmured against his lips, and he laughed.

Ach, ja, surely God was very good.

And if there was an ache in Rebecca's heart to know happiness and love like this, well, God knew all about that, too. Difficult and confusing as it was sometimes, she had to leave her future in His capable hands.

CHAPTER 18

New Birth Sunday

*R*ebecca's stomach was tied in knots as the bishop finished the story of Philip and the Ethiopian eunuch, signaling that the ritual of baptism was about to begin. There was no reason to be nervous, she told herself, her head bowed. She wanted this. She had made her choice ages ago, when she turned twenty-one and knew in her heart that her *Rumspringe* was over.

But still. In front of the entire *Gmee*, sitting hushed in the gravity of the moment on their backless benches in the Yoder living room.

Breathe.

Next to her, Malena's clammy hand reached for hers. A faint tremor ran through it. They'd sat together in church all their lives, being, of course, exactly the same age. Somehow it was comforting to know that gregarious, talented Malena was nervous, too. That Rebecca wasn't the only one. On the bench in front of them, Sara's head was bowed, her hands clutched together in her lap and her elbows pressing her sides, as if she were unconsciously holding herself together.

Rebecca couldn't see her brother Joshua over there on the men's side, but the fact that he was here at all was something of a miracle. This time last year, he'd been ... spring skiing at Whitefish with the Madison boys? She couldn't remember. It didn't matter, anyway. All that would be washed away in the waters of baptism, never to be brought up again in this life or the next. During their fifth baptism class the bishop had reminded him that once he was a member of the church, he would be eligible to be called to the ministry. The thought of scapegrace Joshua falling under the lot and possibly becoming a deacon or minister (or a bishop!) was almost too much for a sister's mind to comprehend.

For Joshua, it had been a moment of humility as the gravity of his choice washed over him. But for Rebecca, seeing his humility was an encouragement. It was the product of a spirit that had submitted to God, and her last tiny worry that he might throw over the traces and run had disappeared.

On Friday night, Little Joe and the ministers had come over to the Circle M after supper for the *Unterricht*, giving the four of them final counseling before the step they would take. Little Joe had read the eighteen articles of the Dordrecht Confession aloud one last time, answered a few last questions, and then to Rebecca's surprise, offered them all the opportunity to change their minds.

"If you are having second thoughts," he'd said gently, "there is no shame in waiting for a time, until your heart is convicted and your mind is made up. These are weighty matters, with eternal consequences. No one will blame you."

None of them had backed out. And Joshua's gaze had been steady as a rock as he'd shaken his head.

There was another reason for her nerves this morning that had nothing to do with her family. At the back was a wheelchair, and seated in it was Andrew King, his parents on either side, no doubt sending prayers of thanks to God that he was well enough for the clinic's van to bring him here. Today of all days. She shouldn't begrudge him that. What better place for him? But ... he and she would be under the eye of the entire *Gmee* with the knowledge of the ridiculous misunderstanding she had caused. Surely they wouldn't think he was here for her...?

But no. She couldn't think about that. One, it was prideful. And two—

Little Joe said, "There are four persons among us who wish to take the step of baptism."

She could hardly breathe. And her fingers were turning white from her twin's grip.

"Sara Fischer, Malena Miller, Rebecca Miller, and Joshua Miller, will you please come before us."

Her knees were shaking, but somehow they supported her as she walked to the front, and stood side by side with the others in order of age. Malena was ten minutes older, so she stood on Rebecca's right, with Joshua on her left.

"Please kneel."

They sank to their knees on the plank floor and bowed their heads.

The bishop gazed at them solemnly. "Can you also confess with the Ethiopian eunuch, 'Yes, I believe that Jesus Christ is the Son of God'?"

One after the other, they answered, "Yes, I believe that

Jesus Christ is the Son of God." Rebecca could hardly hear Malena's reply, so constricted with nerves her throat seemed to be.

Little Joe went on, "Do you also recognize this to be a Christian order, church, and fellowship under which you now submit yourself?"

That was the easy one. *"Ja,"* they answered.

"Do you renounce the world, the devil with all his subtle ways, as well as your own flesh and blood, and desire to serve Jesus Christ alone, who died on the cross for you?"

Joshua was the first to say, *"Ja,"* before his sisters and his intended chimed in.

The bishop took a slow breath before asking the final question. "Do you also promise before God and His church that you will support these teachings and the *Ordnung* with the Lord's help, faithfully attend the services of the church, help counsel and work in it, and not forsake it, whether it leads you to life or death?"

"Ja, I promise," they said, one after the other. Rebecca's heart lifted as with that single sentence, she committed her life to Christ and his church.

"Let us pray," Little Joe said, and the members of the *Gmee* rose to their feet, heads bowed, while she and the others remained on their knees. When he concluded, there was a rustling and whispering as everyone sat except Little Joe and Calvin Bontrager, Susan's father, who was the deacon.

Rebecca's hands covered her face to indicate her shame-facedness before God, but she knew that Calvin and Little Joe were approaching Sara. Calvin would be carrying a pitcher filled with fresh spring water. A fleeting thought made her wonder if that was why Little Joe had been cleaning the filter in the springhouse. So that the water would be as fresh and clear as God intended it for this moment.

"They that believe and are baptized shall be saved," the bishop began. Rebecca heard the murmured words, the moments of silence as the water was poured, the blessing, and the gentle sound of the bishop's wife giving Sara the holy kiss. Then the same for Malena. And then it was her turn.

She lowered her hands, but her head remained bowed.

"Rebecca Miller, upon your faith, which you have confessed before God and many witnesses, you are baptized in the name of the Father, the Son, and Holy Ghost." With each of the holy names, Calvin tipped water into the bishop's cupped hands, and it trickled cold over the crown of Rebecca's head.

Then he offered her his hand and helped her rise. Sadie, standing beside her husband, leaned in to give her the holy kiss.

When Joshua had been baptized, Little Joe gave him the holy kiss himself, and despite the solemnity of the moment, smiled into her brother's eyes in welcome. It had been a long, hard road, but Joshua's submission now and his willingness to humble himself before *Gott* and the *Gmee* meant that he would have the support not only of his family, but also of the entire community in doing his Father's will.

The bishop included all four of them in his gaze. "You are now no longer strangers and pilgrims on the earth, but fellow citizens with the saints and of the household of God. Go in peace."

Rebecca returned to her seat in a glow of joy, and when she and Malena took their places on the bench and the *Vorsinger* began the hymn, she took her sister's hand. No longer trembling and nervous, instead she felt clean. These were the first moments of a new life, and how glad she was that she could share them with her brother, her sister and her future sister-in-law. At last she understood what Paul had written to the Corinthians.

> *Therefore if any man be in Christ, he is a new creature: old things are passed away; behold, all things are become new.*

THERE WAS something about the fellowship meal that followed a baptism that was just a little different from the others in the course of the Amish year. The four new members of the *Gmee* sat together, enjoying a potluck lunch contributed by nearly every family in the district. Rebecca's family had contributed a big pan of macaroni and cheese, with a layer of ham on the bottom, that would make your eyes roll up in your head, it was so good. It was fattening as could be, but Rebecca loved it. With coleslaw and baked beans and all manner of pickles and desserts, they were enjoying a feast.

Since they were sitting together, it made it easy for members of the *Gmee* to stop by and offer a few words of gladness and support. Never congratulations, for that would be prideful and lessen the importance of the work of the Spirit. But as each one stopped by their end of the table, the glow in Rebecca's heart grew.

"How lucky we are to live here," she confided to Sara, who was sitting opposite with Joshua. "Everyone is so kind."

"And to think that when I left, all I wanted was to run away and never come back," Sara said with a shake of her head. "I saw these folks as judgmental and rigid, when all the time I never realized I was judging myself. Weighing myself on my own scale and finding myself wanting."

Baby Nathan cooed and patted her mouth with one hand, making her laugh.

"He says, 'Judge not and ye shall not be judged,'" Rebecca translated. "Even yourself."

"Good advice," Sara said, and blew kisses into his neck to make him smile. "What a clever boy he is."

Around three o'clock, Joshua took Sara and Nathan back to the ranch, and Mamm and Dat left with baby Deborah as well. Gone were the days when the whole family might stay all day, visiting and catching up with their neighbors. Now Mamm needed her rest, and the babies needed their naps.

"I guess that leaves us singles to hold up tradition," Malena said, following Rebecca outside. "Look, there's Ruby and Alden Stolzfus. I'm going to go talk to them."

Rebecca did not mention that maybe Alden might want to talk to Ruby alone. Saying things like that to Malena never did any good—she assumed people would be as glad to talk with her as she was with them. Maybe they were. But Rebecca was waiting for the day when Malena fell for someone and realized how precious a stolen moment of conversation could be.

"Rebecca, I was hoping to catch you."

She turned in surprise to see Arlon King pushing Andrew along the concrete path around the house. There was a wider pad poured behind the house where the Yoder women hung out the laundry, and Andrew waved her over.

"*Ischt okay, Dat.* I'll just talk a little with Rebecca until you and Mamm are ready." As his father withdrew, Andrew explained, "We have to give the neuro clinic's van driver half an hour's notice." When Rebecca nodded, he went on, "The driver would have stayed for the service if it hadn't been a baptism. But when I explained it was for church members only, he understood."

"The clinic isn't so far away that it's inconvenient to come back," she offered. "Shame he missed lunch, though."

"That macaroni and cheese was my favorite," he said. "I'll marry the woman who made it if she'll promise to make it every day of my life."

She had to laugh. "You're nearly thirty years too late, I'm afraid. It's Mamm's recipe."

"Then I'll settle for one of the girls who helped her." He waggled his eyebrows at her, and she shook a finger at him.

"No starting any more rumors or misunderstandings," she said firmly. "I don't want to go through that again. Even while I'm standing here talking to you, someone is bound to say that we're warming up cold soup."

"Would that be so bad?"

Oh, he was such a flirt. Even after what he'd been through, Andrew King could still command the attention of every woman in the room. Or yard, as the case may be.

He went on, "Not that we had any soup to warm up, if what you tell me is true."

"Oh, it's true," she assured him. "In fact, this is another first —a conversation where you're not in a hospital bed."

Now the flirtation fell away. "You're kidding."

"I'm not." She smiled and gazed over the roof of the barn, where the mountains rose in the distance, forming a fence between their valley and what lay beyond. Colorado. "I was in Amity for the summer, and we never spoke once. It's not your fault—you just never noticed me."

"Now, that can't be true. You're just being modest. I like that about you."

She brushed off the last part. "It is true. We were at three volleyball games, two church meetings, two singings, and a dinner. And at none of those occasions did we ever speak."

Because he was always surrounded, and she was too shy.

"All that, huh? But someone must have introduced us."

"I don't think so. You know how it is. A crowd having fun, everybody talking. It's easy to overlook people."

He shook his head in disbelief. "You make me sound pretty rude."

"I don't mean to." At the time, it had been all she could do to remember her own name, she was so overwhelmed by him. Dizzy from falling head over heels. "I just think you were preoccupied by everyone who wanted to talk with you."

"They couldn't have been more important than you."

"Ach, well, over and done," she said with a shrug.

"But I must have made some impression on you," he persisted. "You recognized me the night of the accident. Saved me. Told them who I was. Right?"

"I did recognize you. After being at the three volleyball games—"

"Two church meetings, dinner, right, right." He laughed. "I'm glad about that." He leaned back in his chair, as comfortable as if it were a sofa and he was about to invite her to sit beside him. "Well, we know each other now, probably better than two people have a right to."

Not nearly as well as she had come to know Noah. Maybe now was an opportunity to rectify that.

"Do you plan to stay on in the business with your brothers?" she asked.

His brows rose at the change of subject. "If they'll have me, once I'm healed."

"Will you go back to Amity? Simeon says he and Noah will be leaving around the middle of May. You probably won't be healed by then, but you seem to be making progress."

"I hope so," he said fervently. "I've had enough of doctors and pills and PT for a lifetime and I only got here Monday."

"PT? Oh, physical therapy. But will you go back?"

He gave his one-shoulder shrug. "I suppose so, if my brothers are. I may not be able to swing a hammer for a while, but there are other things I can do."

She was collecting facts, but she couldn't say she was getting to know him. This was much more difficult than talking with Noah. And she wasn't even distracted by Andrew's looks. Maybe she was getting used to him.

"Do you enjoy carpentry?"

"Sure." He gazed at her curiously. "I do a good enough job, I guess. Why?"

She felt a blush burning into her cheeks. "I don't know. It seems Noah wants to try out cowboying. I wondered if you'd ever wanted to do anything else."

With a snort of amusement, he said, "Sure, I've wanted to try things. We all do. But I'm a competent carpenter and we need the money, so why not do what I'm good at? My brother, now ... well, I'd buy a ticket to see him riding and roping." He laughed. "He's never even been to a rodeo, that I know of. What bee got into his bonnet that suddenly he wants to be a cowboy?"

Something about the question rubbed Rebecca the wrong way, like brushing upward on a horse's coat instead of in the direction it naturally lay. "Can he ride a horse?"

"I have no idea. If he can, I've never seen it. Horses aren't for riding where we come from. They're for work."

"Cutting horses are for work, and we ride them," she pointed out. "But not for pleasure. They have a job to do, like any other animal or person on the ranch."

He straightened in his wheelchair, interested now. "Can you ride a horse?"

"Sure. All of us can. We all have to help when we trail the cattle up or down the mountain. Every hand is needed to keep a couple hundred cows and calves from spreading all over creation until they're supposed to. Especially when part of the trail is the highway."

Andrew looked at her doubtfully. "You're a cowboy? Girl," he corrected himself.

"I'm a cattleman's daughter," she retorted. "If my father needs my sister and me on a horse to help get the cattle ready for market, then that's what we do. All of us are involved—though Mamm helps by feeding the crew at the end of the day. She'll ride if she has to, but she'd rather not. And now with Deborah—"

Andrew had opened his mouth to say something else, but Noah came around the corner of the house. "There you are. Dat says to tell you the van will be here in a few minutes."

"That's too bad," Andrew said. "Rebecca and I were having an eye-opener of a conversation."

"What about?" Noah asked easily, joining them. "It's not too cold out here for you?"

"No, and don't treat me like an invalid," Andrew said, frowning. "We were talking about cowboying. Rebecca says she rides the trail like any good rancher's daughter."

"I expect she does," Noah said. "I'd sure like to stay an extra week or two and see how it's done. Tagging and branding and trailing and the like."

"Can you even ride a horse?" Andrew may have wanted to know, but his tone was challenging.

Noah shrugged. "We built a barn at the Lost Creek Ranch last year. I think you were out on a different job. One of the hands was from Whinburg Township. Samuel, his name was. He gave me some practice."

Andrew's jaw went slack in pretend astonishment. "And here you accused *me* of keeping secrets."

"I didn't think anyone would care one way or the other. And not saying anything about a couple of days on a horse isn't quite the same as not saying anything about being engaged." He glanced at Rebecca. "Of course, now we know why you didn't. Because you weren't."

"Not then," his brother snapped.

"Not to me," Rebecca said hastily, "but what about that girl? The one who left you in the river. Have you been able to remember anything about her?"

She didn't know what made her bring that up. Maybe because he was teasing Noah, and the teasing had an edge that could leave a cut.

"What girl?" Andrew looked mystified. "What are you talking about?"

"The night of your accident," Rebecca said, "the two of you passed me in a car, going really fast. You spun out at the intersection and she was screaming at you about something. I don't know what. But you were so drunk that you tried to get out of the car while it was still moving, and you were thrown out and over the bank."

He just stared at her as if he'd never heard any of this before. Had no one told him?

Noah glanced at her and said, "Rebecca told me afterward that this woman, whoever she was, didn't stop to see if you were okay. She just gunned the car up the hill and disappeared."

"That's why I went down there. I thought you were a dog." She smiled at him, feeling as though she ought to apologize for that. "It was dark. I didn't know then that it was you. I just knew I had to get an unconscious man somewhere safe before he froze to death."

"Then at the fire station, she recognized you," Noah finished. "And you know the rest."

Andrew made a motion with his hand. *Back up.* "So I was with someone—an *Englisch* woman, obviously—in a car. And she was screaming?"

"Screaming at you," Rebecca said. "It sounded like you were having a fight."

"Some fight," he said. "And this red car, what did it look like?"

Noah went still. Glanced at Rebecca.

"I don't know cars," she said slowly. "I can tell the difference between a car and a truck. That's it. But Andrew, I never said what color it was."

He looked into the distance—or maybe his memory—as if he was trying to hear something far away. "You must have."

"I couldn't. Like I said, it was dark. I had the buggy lights on, but she was gone by the time I got Hester stopped."

"A red car," Noah said. "Maybe your memory just shook something loose. That's a good sign, *nix?*"

"Did you see the driver?" Andrew ignored his brother's question. "What did she look like?"

"*Neh*," Rebecca said. "It all happened so fast, and then I forgot about her while I was dragging you up the bank."

"I still can't believe you managed that," Noah said to her with a quiet smile. "But I'm glad you did."

She smiled back. "With God all things are possible."

"But this girl," Andrew said, frowning. "Driving a red car. The only *Englisch* girl I know who had a red car was in Breckenridge. She was a ski instructor. But I haven't seen her since I went home."

"That you know of."

"Oh, I'd know that," Andrew said with an inflection that told Rebecca this ski instructor had been the kind of woman a man remembered. "We dated for a while. But then I left."

But had he gone back? Say, for a month when he was supposed to be in Montana working on his parents' house?

It would all come to him in time. Until then, it was none of her business, and here was Arlon King to push Andrew's chair to the clinic's van. Rebecca smiled in farewell and drifted away to find Malena, but only Noah looked up long enough to smile back.

CHAPTER 19

*S*o his brother had remembered a red car, and a woman who might have owned it. The two thoughts niggled at Noah over the next several days. Woven into them was the unwelcome memory of Andrew and Rebecca out back of the Yoder house, talking like old friends. It was difficult for Noah to stomach the possibility that the engagement-that-never-was might well become the-engagement-that-could-be.

Surely not.

Rebecca might once have had feelings for Andrew, but they weren't the kind that you built a lifetime on. She'd freely admitted that it had been a crush—a powerful one, maybe, but without the nourishment of actually getting to know him, it must eventually dwindle away. Which led him to the real reason the friendly little scene on Sunday had so disturbed him. The getting-to-know-you part had begun. When Andrew got to know Rebecca better, Noah had no doubt she'd be haunting his thoughts and dreams the way she did Noah's. But when Rebecca got to know Andrew?

There lay waters more dangerous than an icy river.

Because when Andrew finally recovered his memory, would they find out that he'd concealed his return to his relationship with the woman in the red car? How was Rebecca going to handle that? And what was more, would Andrew's relationship with God and the church stand up to that missing month? Maybe Rebecca could forgive an old flame that had flared up and ended before she'd met Andrew again. But could she face a third backslide to an *Englisch* life, and trust that his heart was faithful now?

As Noah painted the cupboards in the farmhouse kitchen, the questions, the uncertainties, bothered him as mercilessly as a flock of midges.

By Thursday, the kitchen walls were textured and painted and the cabinets re-hung. They'd even stripped, sanded, and re-varnished the plank floor until it glowed as good as new. As Noah stood in the doorway, he felt a sense of satisfaction that now Mamm could bring in her cookware and stock the pantry. Once their family dining table was in and the old-fashioned blue checkered oilcloth laid over it, it would really feel like home.

Upstairs, the rhythmic swish and scrape of the trowel told him Simeon was enjoying himself. Mudding a wall was the part Sim liked best, when the labor was nearly done and he could take a little time to do a craftsman's job on the finishing work.

Noah heard the sounds of a horse and buggy outside, and stepped out on the porch. The breeze was still cool, but in it he smelled a scent of green from the shoots springing up through the dead mat of last year's grass, and leaves unfurling on the branches around the house. He felt a tingle of surprise and happiness as first Rebecca hopped down and then Malena, who had held the reins.

"We've brought the rest of the window quilts," Malena called as she secured the horse. "Any chance you've been able to hang the rods inside the frames?"

"They're ready and waiting," Noah said with a smile of welcome.

The twins emerged from the back of the buggy with neat armloads of the short, narrow quilts made to fit the sash windows, and carried them into the house. He heard them greet Sim as they got started hanging them in the completed bedrooms. While the dual-pane windows would keep out nearly all the cold, the window quilts would make sure that the rooms stayed warm and snug, especially at this unpredictable time of year.

Noah was considering moseying upstairs to see if he could be of help when the sound of car tires on gravel—an entirely different sound from Amish buggy wheels—made him return to the door. Another surprise—it was the neuro clinic's van, which could only mean one thing.

"Sim!" he hollered up the stairs. "Andrew's here!"

His parents and the girls, even Aendi Annie clutching her shawl around her, came pouring out the door of the *Daadi Haus*. Mamm flung her arms around Andrew as soon as his wheelchair was lowered to the ground on the elevator platform on the back of the van.

"Andrew! *Mei Sohn!* Why didn't you send word?"

"I didn't know Aendi Annie's cell phone number, and besides, I know you like a surprise." He grinned up at their mother. "I came to see how the work is progressing."

"I'll be back in two hours, Mr King," the driver said, and

climbed into his van. Belatedly, Noah saw that there were two other patients in the van, clearly also anxious to visit family and friends.

"Well, come in and see," Dat said. "We'll be moving in soon, much to Annie's relief, I'm sure."

"Never believe it. It's like old times," their aunt said, her wrinkles falling naturally into a smile. "I love my Kate's family around me."

Dat wheeled Andrew over, where they abruptly realized that somehow, no one had taken a wheelchair into account when they had repaired the front steps and wraparound veranda.

"I'll go get a ramp," Noah said.

"*Neh*, don't." Andrew grinned. "I have something to show you. Hand me that crutch."

Noah pulled a crutch from the back of the chair, and with only a little difficulty, Andrew rose to his feet. Mamm gasped. Dat and Noah both moved in on either side of him as, one at a time, he mounted the steps without their assistance.

"I've been practicing stairs all week," he told them when he reached the door. "The doctor is amazed at my recovery. My muscles remember a little more each day, and I couldn't wait to show you."

It was amazing. Though the fractured leg was in a cast, and the crutch supported him, the other leg looked to Noah to be practically as good as new. It was bearing his brother's weight.

"You're just in time to help," Dat told him. "Noah and I will bring in the kitchen table and some chairs, and you can sit there and unpack boxes for your mother."

"That I can do," Andrew said. "Whose buggy is that outside? Do we have company?"

"Andrew!" Rebecca exclaimed from the archway. "I thought I heard your voice, and couldn't imagine how you got here."

Dat told her what they were going to do, and she and Malena promptly offered to help. Fifteen minutes later, they were seated at the table with Andrew while Noah and his sisters began carting in boxes. They'd been stored in the barn, waiting for just this occasion. Rebecca quietly organized them into a process, with Mamm and Patricia at the end of it, stowing things where they belonged and talking over what to do with things like mixing bowls when there wasn't an island with a pastry top like they had in Kansas.

"I remembered some more," Andrew said to Rebecca as he unwrapped coffee mugs. "After I left Amity on the bus, I got off at Whitefish."

"Good for you," she said. "Whitefish isn't so far away. Do you remember anything after that?"

Whitefish was a ski area where lots of *Englisch* folks came for spring skiing, Noah remembered. And Andrew had known a woman with a red car who had been a ski instructor. That did not bode well.

But Andrew shook his head. "Not so far. Just flashes. But if my brain is remembering more about moving my leg every day, then maybe it will remember more of that, too."

"But Whitefish?" Dat said, looking puzzled. "Why there?"

"The train goes through there on its way to Libby, Dat," Noah said. "Remember, we looked at the schedule before we decided the van was more economical."

"But why get off there?" Simeon asked, washing his hands at the pristine new sink and then realizing too late there were no towels. He would have wiped his hands on his pants, but Malena handed him a towel that a glass salad bowl had been wrapped in. "That's what I don't understand. Why not just stay on the bus until Libby? Or Mountain Home, even? It goes right through here. We saw it the other day."

Andrew frowned, but whether it was Sim's questions or because he couldn't remember any of the answers, Noah couldn't tell.

"Your guess is as good as mine," Andrew finally said, then turned to Rebecca. "So, what brings you girls over here just in time to see me?"

Malena explained about the window quilts.

"But we should be going pretty soon," Rebecca added. "With Daniel and Lovina's wedding a week from today, you would not believe the scrubbing going on up at the ranch. I'm sure my father will be washing down the cows in the barn by the end of it."

"I'm just enjoying the sight of Zach and Adam wiping down the log beams in the great room. One ... log ... at a ... time." Malena giggled, and it was hard not to smile along with her. "That's a lot of logs."

"And they're all up near the ceiling," Rebecca said with a grin that held mischief and not a little satisfaction at her brothers' plight.

"Logs—ceiling—" Andrew blinked.

"Did you remember something else, son?" Mamm turned from the silverware drawer.

"Ja, I think so. A cabin? Or maybe the lodge at Breckenridge." Again that frown. "This is so strange. Maybe I should just keep my mouth shut until it all comes back and I have a complete story to tell."

"It's a bit like a jigsaw puzzle," Rebecca suggested. "One piece at a time, but you don't know where they fit."

"It's not like that at all," he said curtly.

Noah nearly snapped at him not to be so rude, but too late. Rebecca withdrew in that way she had. She didn't vanish from the table, but she reminded him of a stone you knew was there in the creek, but water flowed right over it so you almost couldn't see it. You'd never really see her if you didn't know she was there.

Not long afterward, the Miller twins rose to leave. Noah walked them out to their buggy.

"I'm sorry about Andrew," he said in a low voice, touching Rebecca's arm to prevent her climbing in just yet. "He didn't need to take that tone with you."

"I'm sure he didn't mean to." Her head in her away bonnet was bowed. "Maybe I was too forward. Presuming to know what he thinks."

Did Andrew think? Really think? Or did he just barrel through life, having a good time, enjoying himself, and leaving broken hearts strewn in his wake?

"It's impossible for you to be too forward," he said softly. "Not someone as gentle and kind as you."

The bonnet tilted up and suddenly he was falling into that clear gaze the way a lark falls up into the summer sky.

"That's the nicest thing anyone has ever said to me," she said.

"I could say a lot more, but I don't want to make you blush."

To his amazement, the color he was expecting to bloom in her cheeks ... didn't. "I blush at everything. Mamm says it will wear off when I find the place God means for me."

At my side. The words came to his lips so quickly he had to bite them back.

The truth came to his heart simultaneously, leaving him reeling and unable to say another word as she climbed into the buggy.

As Malena shook the reins over Hester's back and they rolled out of the yard, Noah faced the truth that had been hovering so close it was a wonder he hadn't seen it before.

She belonged at his side. And he belonged at hers.

With a conviction so pure yet so unmistakeable it had to come from *Himmel* itself, all his worries and jealousies and fears fell away. Rebecca would never be happy with Andrew. *Gott* had brought Noah here to this valley for her and her alone. And no matter what, he had to stay and see if he might win her heart and her love the way she had won his.

It would come between him and his brothers, each for different reasons. He knew that already. But this certainty, this whisper of rightness inside him would not be denied.

THE NEXT TWO days passed in a whirlwind of work and preparation. When off Sunday finally came, Rebecca sank into its quiet with relief and a prayer of thanks to *der Herr* for designating the first day of the week a day of rest. In the morning, they always gathered in the living room for prayers and Scripture reading. They were making their way through the Bible, each person reading a couple of verses as they went around the room. This morning, along with Daniel's bass, she had the happiness of hearing Lovina's gentle alto and Joel's piping treble. He did well with the Old Testament passages, though it would have been considerably more difficult if they'd been deep in the begats and he had to struggle with all those names.

After a simple lunch, Mamm took a few minutes to rest with Deborah before they heard the first of the buggies in the lane bringing Sunday visitors.

"At least today the house is spotless," Malena whispered as they peeked out the big window at the sound of wheels on gravel. "Oh! Look, it's the Kings, and they've brought Andrew."

"It's a lucky thing he can manage the stairs as well as he can," Rebecca said. Though usually if there was someone in a wheelchair or healing from an injury, Dat and one of the boys would simply carry the person up and into the house. No visitor to the Circle M was ever made to feel that they were unwelcome, or that the Millers were unprepared to do all they could to make them feel comfortable and capable.

The thump of the crutch on the steps told them Andrew was seeing himself to the deck and from there to the front door. When the family flooded into the living room, his jaw dropped as he looked around him, then out at the view. Their furnishings were simple and uncluttered so that the first thing a visitor saw was God's work.

"I've never seen anything like it," Andrew said after everyone had greeted each other and Sara and Malena had gone to the kitchen to lay out the cookies and cake they'd prepared yesterday. "This view. It's amazing."

"My father says no fancy decorations can hold a candle to God's handiwork," Rebecca told him. "Even though he and Meadowlark built this house, he'd rather people looked at *Gott*'s creation than anything he's done."

"I'd like to build houses like this," Andrew said, taking in the plank-over-log walls and the open trusses above. "Plain old frame houses are boring."

"Plain old frame houses keep us in food and tools," Simeon reminded him. "But I'll agree that a house like this is a whole different animal."

"If we stayed here in the Valley, maybe we could get some experience with it," Noah suggested. His voice seemed to Rebecca to be intentionally light, so that Simeon would know he wasn't serious.

"That idea and a dollar will get you a cup of coffee at the Bitterroot Dutch Café," Sim responded in the same light tone.

So much for floating the possibility, Rebecca thought, as Noah subsided.

Andrew nudged her. "How about you show me the view from the deck?"

"It's the same view," she pointed out. After he had shut her down the other day about his memories, she wasn't sure how to hold a conversation with him now. The last thing she wanted was to be humiliated like that again.

Humility was something to be striven for. Humiliation was, as Sim might say, a whole different animal.

"I'd still like to see it," Andrew said. "Come on, grab a sweater. It's almost warm out."

She pulled on the black sweater with the pretty rounded collar and the cables down the front that Mamm had made her, and let them out the back door. From here, the shoulder of the hill rose behind them.

"Mamm keeps all these pots close to the house for herbs and flowers that do better in shelter," she said. "You can't see the big garden from here, but it's below, past the barn, where the soil is rich from the river."

"That's great," he said, by which she understood he wasn't all that interested in women's affairs like gardens.

That was all right, she supposed. Her brothers were only interested in the garden when food was coming out of it. The rest of the time, when Mamm called on them for heavy work like turning over the soil in the spring and repairing the deer fencing, they moaned and groaned about how that wasn't ranch work.

She pointed up the hill. "Up there is a box canyon that my—"

"I didn't really come out here to get a guided tour," he said with the smile that had made her heart turn over in Colorado, when it had been directed at other girls. Now it was hers alone. But somehow the words that went with it took the charm out of it.

He moved closer to her at the rail, his crutch in his right hand and his left side warming hers. "I came to tell something. Or ask, I suppose I should say," he amended. "Doesn't do to tell girls what to do, does it?"

"Only if you're their husband," she said. "And even then you'd speak as you would to your helpmate, not your servant."

He grinned. *"Ja.* Exactly." Then the smile fell away and he captured her gaze. "Rebecca—the truth is—I'd like to court you."

The words went through her like a bolt of lightning, leaving singed emotions in their wake.

"I know I'm supposed to ask one of your brothers to speak for me, but why be old-fashioned when you're the girl who saved my life? You've seen me at my worst—in a way no other woman has. What I want now is for you to see me at my best."

She didn't reply. Words had flown her brain as surely as the sparrows flew away from the barn cats.

"They're going to discharge me on Tuesday," he went on. When she looked up in surprise, he said, "The doctor is happy with my progress. He says if the tests they do tomorrow show as much improvement as the PT has, they'll let me go." His smile flashed again. "I hope you don't mind dating someone on crutches. We won't be going on any hikes for a while, or skiing, but I'm pretty sure I can drive you home from singing."

"We don't ski," she said.

"What?"

"Here. The *Ordnung* forbids skiing, especially for women. It's not modest."

"Well, sure. The *Ordnung* in Colorado forbids it, too, though I don't think any of the *Youngie* have tried it in all the time there's been a church there. Not even on *Rumspringe*."

"But you have."

He nodded. "It's amazing. There's nothing like being up on top of a mountain, and then flying down it like some kind of eagle."

"That was when you were living *Englisch*."

Another nod.

"Will you live *Englisch* again, do you think?"

The smile fell from his face and he moved just enough so that her right side felt cool. "What kind of question is that?"

"It's a reasonable one to ask of someone who has jumped the fence twice."

"And come back twice," he said, as though she'd forgotten.

"Do you think I'm going to court you and then jump the fence a third time?"

Her stomach trembled at her own effrontery, but she had to say it. "Anna May Helmuth would know that answer better than I."

"Whoa." He sounded winded. "You don't pull any punches, do you, for a girl who's so meek and mild."

Not someone as gentle and kind as you, Noah's voice whispered in her mind.

"It seems like a reasonable question," she said.

"Then the answer is *neh*, of course I don't plan to live *Englisch* again. Would you feel better if I'd been baptized with you all last Sunday?"

"That would have been hard, since you haven't had classes and you live in another district."

He chuckled. "You're so literal. What I meant was, if I were to commit to baptism classes, could I court you?"

She shook her head. "Andrew, first of all, you commit to baptism for yourself, not anyone else. And second of all, your brothers expect you to go back to Colorado with them. We already talked about this."

"I bet Noah will talk Sim into staying for the branding and all that. And if he does, I'll stay, too. So, what do you think?"

Once again, everything they'd said was all about him. Not once had he asked about her feelings. Her thoughts. What she wanted—other than his courting her.

And besides that, he'd revealed a strange kind of impracticality. What man would court a woman when he wasn't sure he'd be staying? Was she just someone to entertain him and make him feel wanted for the next month or two? Just long enough for the Amish grapevine to really start speculating—at which point he'd climb on a bus and vanish from her life?

And then there was the secret she'd been keeping since Friday.

"I was in Mountain Home the other day," she said. "And I saw that red car again."

He froze, his elbows on the rail. She doubted he even breathed. Then, "You did?" His chest rose and fell on a big intake of breath. "Are you sure?"

"I'm sure it was the same one. Not because I saw it clearly that night, but because I recognized the racket it made with its engine. I asked the *Englisch* man in the candle shop what kind it was, and he said it was a vintage—"

"Firebird," he said on a note of wonder. "How did I know that?"

"Your memory is coming back."

"I wish it would remember useful things, like where I was all that time."

"It will. But the point is, that woman seems to be back in town. She might even be looking for you. If you're serious about courting anyone, then you have to clear the air with her. Find out the missing pieces."

"And then we can be together?"

She felt as though she were on the edge of a cliff. If anyone said a single word, she would tip over and fall.

"Rebecca?"

She didn't fall. She stepped out. On purpose.

"*Neh.* I don't think that would be a *gut* idea," she said. How strange it was to think that another dream had just come true, and it was now the last thing she wanted. "I don't think we're very well suited."

He stared at her in surprise, as though no one in his entire life had ever said no to him. No woman, at any rate. Except maybe his mother.

"I think it would be foolish to begin courting when your life isn't here," she went on steadily. "I like you, and every night I pray for your healing. But I don't have those feelings for you, Andrew."

"Not any more, you mean." He seemed to be trying to recover. "I know you did. You cared for me, once."

"I still do. The way a friend cares. But I want real love. The kind you build a marriage on. I want what my parents have together, thirty years on."

"And you don't think you'll have that with me." His voice sounded a little flat.

She shook her head.

"Can you find that with someone else? Like my brother Noah? Is that who you're really talking about?"

Was it? No, it couldn't be. Noah was going to leave just as surely as Andrew was.

But yet … after their rocky beginning, who had stood by her like a friend? Who had talked with her so easily it was like talking to family? Who spent more time getting to know her than he did talking about himself? Who didn't need to talk about himself, because his actions spoke louder than words.

"Uh-huh," Andrew said, answering his own question. "I knew it. I *knew* something was going on with you two. There had to be a reason I always saw you together."

She looked him in the eye. "This isn't about Noah. It's about you, and doing something about that woman in the red car. Until you close things with her—which is obviously what she's come back for—you can't move on. Can't find out for true what God's will is for you."

"You sound so certain," he said, trying to make a joke of it.

"I am," she said simply. She turned toward the door to see Noah standing on the threshold, looking as though a lightning bolt had just hit him, too. She spoke over her shoulder to Andrew. "I hope you find your way back."

But whether she meant back to the Circle M or back to God, she never got a chance to clarify. For Andrew had seen Noah, too. He grabbed his crutch and hobbled toward the door, shouldering his brother out of the way. The door closed on both of them, leaving Rebecca alone outside.

In a flood of relief, she took the opportunity God had just given her. She ran down the back steps and headed up the hill. If ever she needed the sweet solace of Mammi's orchard, it was now.

CHAPTER 20

There were even more yellow glacier lilies blooming, with the warmer days they'd been having. They were scattered along the trail and in the grass in sheltered spots. Rebecca reached the mouth of the box canyon and drew a breath of awe.

"Look at you," she said to her old friend the Macintosh, touching the swelling buds that looked ready to burst into bloom any moment. "You're going to look like an *Englisch* bride, aren't you, all white and lacy, by the time Lovina says her vows to our Daniel on Thursday."

She rambled all the way down the middle aisle formed by the two rows of trees. Several varieties of apple bloomed at the same time, but the ones in the back left corner here were more leisurely. When they finally came, the blossoms were thick on the gnarled and crabbed branches.

"We late bloomers stick together, don't we?" she said, patting the cool bark of its trunk. "We're always a surprise to the people around us."

"Isn't that the truth," came a voice from behind her.

Was she forward for hoping he would come? For expecting him, almost? She turned to see Noah under the next to last tree, inspecting the tight buds like she was.

"How much did you hear?" she asked.

"I opened the door and heard you talking about skiing."

She nodded. "So almost all of it."

"Are you angry? I'm sorry I eavesdropped, but—" He stopped. "No, I won't say *but*. There's no excuse."

"I'm not angry. It saves my having to remember it all to tell you." She smiled at his surprise. "It's funny. Ever since the night of the accident, all my dreams have come true. Except now I don't want any of them." She gave a chuckle of disbelief. "Here was Andrew, asking if he could court me, and all I could think of was that red car, and the racket it made in town."

"So she's back."

"I don't know for certain it's her, but if it is, Andrew needs to see her and get himself straightened out."

"I suppose the sheriff wouldn't be interested in knowing she drove away from an unconscious, injured man?"

"He probably would, but I'm not about to call him."

"*Neh*, nor me."

The less their people had to do with *Englisch* law enforcement, the better. Most of the district were on good terms with the sheriff, and everyone came out to the auction that helped fund the volunteer fire department. But accusing someone and bringing charges were not the Amish way.

"*Gott* will deal with that woman's heart," she added after a moment. "And Andrew must deal with his own."

"I've been dealing with mine," he said.

Her own heartbeat went from a walk to a trot in a second. "Have you?"

"I'm going to talk to Simeon," he said, joining her under the old tree and leaning a shoulder on a horizontal branch. "About staying for the ... what do you call it?"

"Spring turnout," she said with a smile. "And all the work that goes with it."

"And after that, I'll tell him that I want to stay in this valley. For good."

She gazed at him while the breeze toyed with her *Kapp* strings.

"I want to live here," he said simply. "Work here. I don't want to walk away from Mamm and Dat and the girls. Especially if Andrew—" His throat seemed to close.

"Leaves again," she finished softly. "That was my greatest reason for turning him away. I simply ... couldn't trust him with my heart. That sounds very hard, but I just couldn't."

"Because he hasn't trusted God with his," Noah said, quietly, almost as though he didn't want the trees to hear.

"Maybe that's it." His understanding released the little weight of guilt she'd been carrying. "I thought I might have been too selfish, or too hard to please. But you've seen it. That's what has been bothering me."

"And yet Mamm ... she gives him her heart, her trust, every time he comes back. And every time, he breaks it and leaves her with nothing but memories."

"But would you want her to do anything else?" she asked him. "Isn't that the nature of a mother's love—to wait, to hope, to trust that God will bring the lost sheep back to the fold?"

He nodded, slowly, unwillingly.

"I think of my own mother, and how she waited for Joshua. Even when my brothers closed themselves off to him and my father would go out to the barn to weep as though

Josh had already gone, she never gave up. She'd never give up on any of us. And look. Josh found Sara, and now he's baptized, and they're planning to be married in the fall. Mamm trusted God to love him back to the fold, and He did."

"You're right," he said. "I need to be more like that. To love him back to *Gott*'s family, too. Not to feel sorry for Mamm for loving him that way, but to live by her example. Because she's living the example of Jesus, isn't she?"

"Easier said than done, I'll admit," Rebecca said with a rueful smile. "But it's the trying that counts. Trying with His help."

"And you're not going to take your own advice, and try to let my brother court you?" Noah's brown eyes twinkled.

"Not me. I'm not his mother or his brother. I told him how I felt, and it was true, and now it's done."

"I heard what he said. About you and me."

Somehow the air had become electric, charged with expectation. As though the very lilies at their feet were listening.

"He was losing his temper. Just guessing about us."

"Andrew may believe the world revolves around him, but he still has his eyes open." He paused. "We could make it true."

A dream had already come true for her today, and she'd walked away from it.

Now a new dream was blooming right here, a little late, like this old apple tree. But wouldn't that make it all the more glorious when it finally did happen?

"Is that what you want?" she whispered.

"It is."

What a miracle—a man who said what he thought. No

games. No making her guess or wonder if she was mistaken. A man as honest and forthright as Dat.

When she didn't reply, he took her cold hand, warming it in his own. "These have been the hardest weeks of my life," he said, his voice a little hoarse. "At first, thinking you were engaged, and wondering how I'd overlooked you, too, back in Amity, and kicking myself for being too late. And then later, once the truth was out, losing hope because I thought you still cared for him."

"And while you were thinking that, I was learning that I didn't care the way I thought I did. Not like—" A hot blush rose and faded in her cheeks at her own forwardness.

"Not like?" he whispered.

"Not like this." She dared to be honest, to look up into his eyes. In those dear brown eyes was an expression she'd never seen before—as though the whole world was opening up to him. "Not like this."

"I've never felt this way, either." Now he'd taken possession of her other hand. His were so warm, so comforting, so … safe. She could put her heart in his care and he would never let it go. "Every time I see you, it's like the sun comes out and all I want is to be in the same room with you, listening and laughing and working with you. Just being together."

"That's how I feel, too," she confessed softly. "When did this happen?"

"For me, it was when we were standing by the buggy the other day," he told her. "You looked up at me, and suddenly it was like the scales fell from my eyes. I just knew. Somehow, I had to find out if there was a chance for me. After all you've been through, I wouldn't blame you for not wanting anything to do with a King ever again."

"Some of them aren't so bad," she teased. "Clara, now, is a real sweetheart."

He laughed. "So once again I'm hoping I'm not too late. Will you let me court you, Rebecca?"

She wrapped her fingers around his and leaned into him. "Oh, it's definitely too late for that."

She heard his breathing stop, and realized that in his humility, he'd taken it the wrong way.

"I already know there isn't another man in the world for me but you," she told him, so there would be no misunderstanding. "Courting seems a bit unnecessary, don't you think?"

His whole body seemed to sag with relief. "But I want to. I don't want to keep it a secret."

She shook her head. "I'm done with secrets. I want everything to be in the light of day, warm and bright, and our families knowing all about it."

"Andrew won't be very happy."

"Andrew has enough to do in his own life. He won't have time for a girl who has more to say to his brother than she ever said to him, even while he was sleeping."

He bent his head until their noses were nearly touching. "And what about that house by the river you told him about? Are you still dreaming about that?"

"That house was a dream," she agreed. "But I want reality, and to know my future pleases God. No matter where that cabin is, as long as my Amish cowboy builds it, I'll be happy."

"Dreams are sweet," he said. "But reality is even better." Smiling, he tilted his head and claimed her lips.

His, she thought as her soul spiraled up through the

branches and into the bright sky with Noah's. *I'm his, for sure and for certain, forever and always.*

AN HOUR LATER, Noah and Rebecca rambled out of the canyon hand in hand. There had been so much to say, so many plans to begin, that it had been a shock to remember that his family would likely be wanting to head home.

The two of them had already decided that they would not hide how they felt from their families. In his heart, Noah was certain, Andrew already knew that a future with Rebecca was no longer possible. And when Simeon heard what Noah had to say, surely he would see that a move to the Siksika Valley would be best for all of them. He would keep his promise to help build Joshua and Amanda's house in Amity, and fulfill their other commitments. Then he'd fly back here, like the Canada geese who knew unerringly where their home was. Even if he took on the responsibility of bringing Aendi Annie's ranch back to life, he could still help Sim with carpentering. And if Andrew stayed, too, why then, the business could stay intact no matter where they were.

They climbed the stairs to the deck and, hearing a strange sound in the yard, walked around the corner of the ranch house to see what it was.

Rebecca gasped and dropped Noah's hand.

A red car, low-slung and growling, was coming down the lane.

"Go get Andrew," Noah said. "How did she know he was here?"

Rebecca was already halfway to the door.

Noah ran down the stairs to the yard and was waiting when the car pulled to a stop. A woman got out and slammed the door. She was tall and slender, dressed in blue jeans and an impractically short plaid jacket that only came to her waist. Her hair was long and black and furled out as the breeze caught it.

"They told me at the clinic Andrew King was out on a visit," she said. "Do you know him?"

"I should," Noah said easily. "He's my brother. And yes, he's here. My family is visiting the Millers, who own this ranch."

"Nice place." She walked toward the stairs. "Up here?"

"Did they tell you his condition? The clinic?"

She halted, her hand on the stair rail. "No. That's private, and I'm not a relative. They just said he was out. I saw the van and followed it."

Belatedly, Noah realized the clinic's van was parked in front of the barn. It must have just got here to pick him up.

"There are a couple of things you might be interested in knowing," he said. "My brother was thrown out of your car that night and if someone hadn't been driving by and dragged him out of the river, he'd have died."

She was silent. She took off her sunglasses to stare at him.

"He spent days under sedation for swelling on the brain. Along with a fractured leg. And a dislocated shoulder."

"I didn't know any of this. Is he going to be all right?"

Reuben Miller had come out on the deck now, and Noah only had a moment. "My brother has amnesia. He doesn't remember what happened that night. Be careful what you say to him."

"Lucky me," he thought he heard her say, but she was already climbing the stairs.

"Come in out of the wind," Reuben said, and Noah followed them inside.

The room was silent. And full of Amish people. And a stranger, who Noah gathered must be the van driver. He was halfway through a piece of gingerbread cake.

The woman halted, and Noah saw her straighten her spine. She was only gazing at one person, who sat upright on the sofa, his leg in its cast stretched out before him and his crutch like a staff in one hand.

"Hullo, Andrew."

"Chelsea," he said. There was a strange expression on his face, as though the sight of her had knocked him sideways. "What are you doing here?"

"I came to find you, of course. We need to talk."

"I've got nothing to say to the person who drove away and left me unconscious in a river."

"I didn't know. We were both drunk. When I figured out what happened the next day, I went back for you, but you were gone."

"If I hadn't been rescued, you'd have found a dead man. Lucky for you I'm both alive and Amish, or you'd be in trouble with the sheriff."

Kate King made a soft sound, and put a cautioning hand on Andrew's shoulder.

"Can we go somewhere private?" Chelsea's gaze moved from one person to another, as though she were counting heads in the audience.

Andrew shook his head. "I've got nothing to say."

She sighed. "All about you. Well, I've got plenty to say."

"Only if it's good-bye. It's over. That old life is over. I'm staying here and I'm staying Amish."

"That's not what you said when you proposed to me at Whitefish. When I said yes."

A ripple of surprise went through the room, and Andrew struggled to his feet without help. He leaned on his crutch, breathing hard. "I don't remember."

"That's no excuse. It still happened. You made a promise."

"Then I'm sorry to say I'm breaking it. Good-bye, Chelsea. I'll walk you to the door."

"You can't do that to me! What about all the money I paid for that cabin? A month in an AirBNB isn't cheap, you know!"

"Is that where I was?"

"Of course that's where you were! You came to find me at Whitefish and moved right in. Two weeks later you're all, Chelsea, please be my wife, and then, okay, maybe the fight on the way here to meet your parents was my fault, but I swear, Andrew, I didn't know you'd fallen out of the car!"

Noah's mind reeled. How must Andrew feel right now, trying to piece together a chain of events that explained so much and yet told them so little?

But the biggest fact of all was the most shocking. He had planned to introduce this woman to the family as his fiancée?

Noah glanced at Rebecca, who was looking as stunned as he felt. Engaged to a worldly woman at the beginning of the month, and asking to court an Amish woman at the end of it? Granted, Andrew hadn't remembered a single detail, but Rebecca's instincts had clearly been sound.

"I'll make you a deal, Chelsea," Andrew said. "I won't tell the sheriff about you leaving me in the snow, and you pick up the tab for the cabin."

Chelsea's face quivered. "Fine. I get it. We're done. But when you decide you can't be Amish again, don't come looking for me. I don't want a man who can't make up his mind. About that, or about anything else."

She spun on one boot heel and went out. Noah closed the door gently behind her.

In a moment, they heard the car fire up, roar as it turned around, and then growl off down the lane into silence. Then, in the distance, even through the windows, they heard the distinctive sound that Rebecca had heard that night. Chelsea gunned the engine down the highway and—hopefully—out of Andrew's life for good.

Down the corridor, little Deborah wailed. As though she had awakened him, Joshua's baby Nathan lifted up his voice in aggravation.

Both Naomi and Sara bolted for the bedroom.

"Well." Rebecca walked over to Noah and took his hand. "I'm glad that's over. Will you help me with the coffee? I'm sure everyone could use a refill, and Andrew might like some of that cake before he has to go back to the clinic."

He smiled into her eyes and nodded. And as she stepped comfortably into the role of hostess, making his family feel calm and Andrew more relaxed, he realized that Rebecca Miller would never disappear in plain sight again.

On the contrary—God had led the two of them to the place where He wanted them. The place where they could grow, and love, and build together. There would be bumps along the way—between Andrew and Sim, there couldn't help but be bumps—but Noah knew that with God, he and Rebecca and their families could overcome anything.

For God was love, and love made everything possible.

EPILOGUE

THE CIRCLE M RANCH

April 29

The *Eck*, the corner table where Daniel and Lovina had been sitting with their *Neuwesitzern*, or side-sitters, for the wedding feast had been lovingly decorated by Adam's twin sisters. Lovina's new wedding china was silver and lavender, so those colors had appeared on every table earlier in the silver pots of purple hyacinth that formed the centerpieces, and now again at supper in the evening in the napkins laid on each plate. Adam and Zach's part as their brother's supporters was nearly over. Now, as the older of the two, all Adam had left to do was this final duty—to call out the names of the single young men and women who would be paired off for supper.

He stood at the top of the stairs, the young men in the bedroom on the right, and the young women in the bedroom on the left. "Rebecca Miller and Noah King."

No surprise there. Adam knew for a fact they'd both asked Lovina to partner them up. Usually a dating couple did, and his sister wasn't shy about being seen in public with Noah. What a difference love had made in the invisible Rebecca. He had known she had a quiet competence and was a steadying influence on Malena, who was a force of nature. But love had given Rebecca a confidence that was tempered with modesty and good sense. And speaking as a brother, Adam was glad that Noah appreciated these things about her. When the announcement of their plans to marry came, Adam and his brothers would welcome him into the family wholeheartedly.

But this next couple on the list was an eyebrow raiser for sure and certain. "Susan Bontrager and Simeon King." Adam couldn't meet Malena's merry eyes or he'd laugh. Poor Sim— he was as good as married now. He just didn't know it yet.

Smiling, Adam went down the list written in Lovina's neat hand, calling out names. Pair by pair, his friends and family members met their dinner partner at the top of the stairs, descending to take their places together at the freshly set tables. Some would stay together for the singing—Adam had no doubt that Simeon's fate was sealed in that department— and some would trade for the partner they really wanted, all in good fun.

Nobody seemed to notice that Adam had not been paired up with anyone. Not even Zach, who had by some fluke been partnered with the bishop's daughter, Ruby, instead of the Yoder girl he'd taken home from singing last church Sunday. Zach, naturally, had more sense than to take the chance of offending anyone in the bishop's family by asking her to trade, and was gamely doing his best to make their supper enjoyable.

Once dinner had concluded and the helpers had taken away the dishes, another team of helpers in the kitchen washed and dried and took them out to the bench wagon, where they would be ready for the next wedding. Adam heard the familiar clatter of china and cutlery as the singing began. But now he had time, under the cover of all the *Youngie's* voices, to be alone with his own thoughts.

Upstairs, laid carefully in a small cardboard box tucked in his closet, was her latest letter. He read them over and over. The first ones from the very beginning of their correspondence had gone soft along the creases, they'd been taken out and read so many times. And then the tone of them had changed. They'd started out chatty and friendly, sharing memories of their meeting the summer before in Whinburg Township, where he'd been helping his cousin Melvin Miller get in the hay crop. But several months in, the letters had become … deeper, he supposed was the best word for it. She had begun to share bits of herself he'd never suspected, and it only made him care for her more. And now … he could hardly believe this latest one. Just thinking about her words made his heartbeat speed up to a gallop.

And now I find that letters and memories are not enough, Adam. This longing in my heart to see you has become as strong as the need for a tree to leaf out in the spring, or for the lemon balm under my window to brave this unpredictable spring and reach for the sun.

I want to reach, too, all the way to Montana. Wouldn't it be wonderful to talk in person? To sit on that big deck you've told me about, and watch the sun go down over the mountains? I've never seen mountains like that. I want to lift up mine eyes unto the hills, and know that my help comes from the heavens I see above them. I hope you'll want to share your heart with me, too.

Oh, listen to me, getting all fanciful when I'm sure you have work to do with the horses and cattle. How I'd love to sit on a fence and watch my friend the cowboy! Maybe someday.

Your sister in Christ,

Elizabeth

Elizabeth Schwartz. Just the thought of her deep blue eyes, her porcelain skin, the graceful way she moved, were enough to make Adam's heart clutch with longing. He had been waiting all his life for a woman as lovely, as wise, as spiritual as Elizabeth—and they were on opposite sides of the country.

He had to do something. She'd set it down in black and white that she wanted to come to the ranch. Would it be so outrageous if he asked Mamm and Dat to extend an invitation? Summer was coming—the ranch would be at its best and there would be lots for them to do.

Something inside him settled into place. A decision.

The sound of singing surged back into his ears and Adam came to himself. "Take Me Home, Country Roads." Well, if that wasn't a sign, nothing was.

Once Daniel and Lovina had begun their wedding visits, Adam would approach his parents. They would say yes, and then he would write.

He had a feeling it would turn out to be the most important letter he would ever send.

THE END

AFTERWORD

I hope you've enjoyed the third book about the Miller family. If you subscribe to my newsletter, you'll hear about new releases in the series, my research in Montana and other states and provinces where the Amish make their homes, and snippets about quilting and writing and chickens—my favorite subjects! Visit adinasenft.com to sign up, and be sure to browse my other Amish novels set in beautiful Whinburg Township, Pennsylvania, beginning with *The Wounded Heart.*

To find out what happens when more than just an envelope arrives for Adam at the Circle M, I hope you'll go on to the fourth book in the Montana Millers series, *The Amish Cowboy's Letter.*

Denki!

—Adina

GLOSSARY

Spelling and definitions, and capitalization of nouns, from Eugene S. Stine, *Pennsylvania German Dictionary* (Birdboro, PA: Pennsylvania German Society, 1996).

Words used:

Aendi: auntie

batzich: crazy

bidde: please

Bischt du okay? Are you okay?

Boppli, Bopplin: baby, babies

Bob: bun; hairstyle worn by Amish girls and women

Bruder: brother

Daadi: Grandfather

Daadi Haus: lit "grandfather house," where older members of the family may live

demut: humble

denki, denkes: thank you, thanks

Dochder, Dochdere: daughter, daughters

Dokterfraa: female herbal healer

Duchly: headscarf

mei Fraa: my wife

der Herr: the Lord

der Himmlischer Vater: the heavenly Father

Englisch: non Amish people, also their language

Gefunnenes: foundling

Gmee: The church, the local Amish congregation

Gott: God

guder mariye: good morning

guder owed: good afternoon

guder nacht: good night

gut: good

Herr, der: the Lord

Himmel: heaven

Huddlerei: confusion

ischt okay: it's okay

ja: yes

Ja, ich komme: Yes, I'm coming

Kapp: prayer covering worn by plain women

Kinner: children

Kumm hier: Come here

Kumme mit: Come with me

Liewi, Liebschdi: dear, darling

Loblied: The traditional second hymn sung in the Amish service

Maedel: maiden, young girl

Maud: maid, household helper

Mamm: Mom, Mother

Mammi: Grandmother

Mei Gott, hilfe mich! My God, help me!

mei Hatz: my heart

mei Sohn: my son

Nachteil: night owl, screech owl

neh: no

nix: short for *nichts*, meaning *is it not* or *ain't so?*

Ordnung: discipline, or standard of behavior and dress unique to each community

Rumspringe: "running around"—the season of freedom for Amish youth between sixteen and the time they marry or join church

Schweschder: sister

Uffgeva: giving up of one's will, submission

verhuddelt: confused, mixed-up

Vorsinger: One who begins the hymns

Was ischt? What is it?

Wie geht's? How goes it?

Youngie: Amish young people 16 years and older

ALSO BY ADINA SENFT

Amish Cowboys: The Montana Millers

"The Amish Cowboy's Christmas" (novella)

The Amish Cowboy

The Amish Cowboy's Baby

The Amish Cowboy's Bride

The Amish Cowboy's Letter

The Amish Cowboy's Makeover

The Amish Cowboy's Home

The Whinburg Township Amish series

The Wounded Heart

The Hidden Life

The Tempted Soul

Herb of Grace

Keys of Heaven

Balm of Gilead

The Longest Road

The Highest Mountain

The Sweetest Song

"The Heart's Return" (novella)

ABOUT THE AUTHOR

USA Today bestselling author Adina Senft grew up in a plain house church, where she was often asked by outsiders if she was Amish (the answer was no). She holds a PhD in Creative Writing from Lancaster University in the UK. Adina was the winner of RWA's RITA Award for Best Inspirational Novel in 2005, a finalist for that award in 2006, and was a Christy Award finalist in 2009. She appeared in the 2016 documentary film *Love Between the Covers*, is a popular speaker and convention panelist, and has been a guest on many podcasts, including Worldshapers and Realm of Books.

She writes steampunk adventure and mystery as Shelley Adina; and as Charlotte Henry, writes classic Regency romance. When she's not writing, Adina is usually quilting, sewing historical costumes, or enjoying the garden with her flock of rescued chickens.

Adina loves to talk with readers about books, quilting, and chickens!
www.adinasenft.com
adinasenft@comcast.net